FLO AND MAUDE
CHRISTMAS CAPERS

BOOKS BY SARAH OSBORNE

FLO AND MAUDE CHRISTMAS CAPERS

SARAH OSBORNE

Copyright 2020 by Sarah Osborne

First Edition: October 2020

ISBN: 978-0-578-74868-9

Imprint: Independently published

Printed in the United States of America

❀ Created with Vellum

To my village:
my beta readers
my 241 Fitness buddies
and all women of a certain age

ACKNOWLEDGMENTS

As always I'm indebted to my beta readers, some of whom read these stories numerous times. They include: Lucy Davidson, Jayne Farley, Alix Joslyn, Mary Louise Klimm, Kathy Mosesian, Laurie Pocius, Lynne Rozsa, Donna Shapiro, Margo Schmidt, and Jean Wentzell.

My writing group, as usual, encouraged me and helped improve my style: Larry Allen, Mike Fournier, BettyAnn Lauria, and Amy Wilson.

I also thank my 241 Fitness group headed by Wendy Bryant for keeping me healthy even during times when we couldn't meet in person.

CONTENTS

MALICE AT THE PALACE

"Never in this establishment, Miss Wellington. Our employees are loyal and law abiding!"

I thought Elizabeth's head might spin when I suggested perfidy at the Palace Hotel. She was the concierge on duty, and we'd known each other for years. A lovely Chinese-American woman, her alabaster complexion reddened as she responded. She looked a little like one of the bright red Christmas ornaments nestled in a bowl on the counter between us.

"Perfidy?" she said.

"No need to get indignant, Elizabeth," I said. "I'm just telling you what I heard. You always say you like to be informed, so I'm informing you. Your daytime and nighttime assistant managers Joe Ryland and Mike Murch are up to no good. I overheard them scheming last night."

All this appeared to be too much for Elizabeth. "Perfidy?" she repeated softly.

I could use a simpler word I assured her, like treachery or deceit, but I never like dumbing down the conversation. "The point is, my dear Elizabeth, your two managers are planning to commit grand larceny and murder."

"How did you know who they were?" Elizabeth asked.

"That's an interesting story. One called the other Joe, as in 'Joe, are you sure about all this? And he responded, 'Mike, you worry too much.' They were both wearing those official jackets your management seems to think are attractive and professional.

"I came down to the front desk. No one was there—I could hear your night deskman snoring in the back room. Behind the desk, a roster was pinned up with the names and designations of each of the management employees scheduled to work over the holidays. They were the only Mike and Joe listed."

An expression that I didn't like passed across Elizabeth's face, a look of patronizing disbelief.

They knew me at the Palace the way everyone knew Eloise at the Plaza, perhaps precisely the same way—as an amusing trouble maker. I'd been coming nearly every Christmas since I was two. First, my father brought me, and later I came on my own. On every visit, I groused about the decorations—there were too many of them or too few, they were garish or too understated. Occasionally, I pulled what I considered a hilarious prank, like when I painted Rudolph's nose a disgusting chartreuse. I was little more than a child at the time.

The hotel calls itself "Boston lodging suitable for royalty," and while I'm not royalty—exactly—I am a Boston Brahmin. Personally, I hate the term because it makes me feel like a prize cow, and my large stature does nothing to dispel that image. My beloved father, however, insisted I embrace my position and use it to do good in the world. He didn't seem to care that people referred to him as Beef Wellington behind his back. I certainly hoped they weren't calling me that.

Elizabeth snapped me to attention. "Is this one of your practical jokes, Miss Wellington?"

"I assure you it is not."

Elizabeth was starting to irritate me.

"I'm simply telling you something is rotten in the state of Denmark."

The red spots on Elizabeth's cheeks grew larger. "If you are not pleased with the service we provide, I will do everything I can to make your stay completely to your liking."

"Good grief, Elizabeth, you young people can be so literal. You cater to my every wish. I have far too much space in the Royal Suite, and I only stay there so I can play the piano at all hours."

She gave me a puzzled look.

Perhaps I should text her. Maybe that would help her focus.

"This is not about me. It's about the fact that someone—a guest here—is in danger of losing her life."

Elizabeth leaned in close to me. "Let's talk somewhere . . . more private," she said. "Give me a moment.

"I have all day. I'm not certain the same can be said for the intended victim."

Elizabeth spoke to the young woman beside her. The woman looked to be about twelve, but then everyone looked about twelve these days. It only mattered when they claimed to be one of my doctors.

Elizabeth led me to a tiny room behind the concierge desk. It was smaller than the coat closet in the Royal Suite, but, of course, the space itself was not the issue. We sat scrunched together on the two small chairs available.

"Is this room soundproofed?" I asked.

Elizabeth stared at me. "I wouldn't think so."

I moved my chair as far back from the door as it would go.

"I'm not paranoid, just concerned about the traffic flow outside this door. Where is the assistant day manager?"

Elizabeth glanced at her watch. "He is probably in the Flower Garden restaurant checking on the service. There have been a few complaints."

"I see. Perhaps if the assistant managers are busy planning a murder, a few things like customer service might get pushed aside."

"Really, Miss Wellington!" She stood, all five feet of her, trying to look indignant.

"Please, sit back down. I believe we can handle this situation between us. We are two intelligent women, and I have my friend here." I took my Remington Derringer out of my Kelly bag and thought Elizabeth might faint.

Kate was forever urging me to buy something smaller like a tasteful Gucci handbag, but if the Kelly bag suited Grace, then it certainly suited me. It held everything I might possibly need, including my Derringer.

"I haven't fired this gun in fifty years," I said, "but I still know how."

"Would you . . .would you mind putting that away?" she asked.

"Certainly, my dear." I slipped it back into my bag. "I only wanted you to realize I'm prepared for anything that might happen, and you know my assistant, Kate Fitzhugh, the one who rescued you from impending disaster four years ago, wasn't it? She's staying with me in the hotel."

"I know I owe you and Kate my life and my career, Miss Wellington, and I know you won't let me forget that." Elizabeth looked younger than her thirty-five years, but as she spoke she aged before my eyes. I thought she might cry, something I always find distasteful.

"I'm not rubbing it in, my dear. We've all had those dalliances that seem so important until we realize the man in question is a scoundrel. Kate just happened to discover a few facts about your boyfriend and save you from a lifetime of misery. And I just happened to know that the former manager at this hotel was looking for a new concierge. It was your hard work that put you in charge."

Elizabeth smiled tentatively. She could read me almost as well as Kate. I rarely brought up old history unless I intended to use it for my benefit.

"So, you must understand, dear Elizabeth, I may ask you to do a few things not strictly by the book. I hate to be crass, but, as you said, you do owe me."

Elizabeth sighed deeply.

"This simply must be handled my way," I said, "discreetly in order to save a life. Is that understood?"

Elizabeth started to nod like a bobble head. I resisted the urge to grab her chin and make her stop.

"Here's what I overheard."

Elizabeth's head miraculously stilled.

"It was two a.m. I couldn't sleep, so I thought I'd go to the Fitness Center for a brief workout. As you undoubtedly know they turn off overhead lights at ten and expect us to find our way with the lighting along the floorboards as if we are on some giant airplane about to crash. Ridiculous and inadequate. You'll get sued if one of your old insomniacs like me breaks a hip in the dark—that much I can tell you.

"Before I got to the Center on the fourth floor, I heard whispering near room 462. I remained in the shadows and saw two men standing very close together. They were so intent on their conversation, they never noticed I was there. Unfortunately, because the entire hallway was so dim, I couldn't see them clearly."

Elizabeth started to do that bobbing thing again, and I wondered if she had developed a new-onset seizure disorder.

"They were talking like schoolboys, and I would have

dismissed the whole thing as some childish practical joke from men who'd had too much to drink. But then disturbing words crept in, like 'an unfortunate death' and 'snatching jewelry like candy.'"

"Did they mention the name of the intended victim?" Elizabeth asked.

"It was a 'she'—that much I got. 'The old bird won't know what hit her.'"

As I said those words I had a most uncomfortable feeling, like the sensation Scrooge had when the ghost of Christmas Future pointed in the direction of a grave. "You do have other old birds staying in this hotel besides me, don't you?"

"Of course," Elizabeth said and then caught herself. "You are not an old bird, Miss Wellington—I didn't mean to imply that."

"Of course I am, but I've seen plenty of white heads around the place. Who else but young techies and old birds could afford these exorbitant prices?" I waved off Elizabeth's protest. "They made reference to the fact that her jewels would disappear at the time of her death."

Once more I felt an unpleasant tingling and couldn't help but finger the emerald and ruby necklace my father had given me on my sixteenth birthday.

"Are you all right, Miss Wellington? Would you like a glass of water?" Elizabeth asked.

"I'm fine. I simply don't want to ignore the obvious. I'm of a certain age, clearly with jewelry worth stealing."

"I've always encouraged you to leave your jewelry in our manager's safe."

"I like to have my things near me," I said. "Are there others like me—wealthy women who are here alone at the Palace?"

"I'd have to check," Elizabeth said. "I really think we must get you a bodyguard while I investigate this matter."

"I have my bodyguard," I said, motioning to the gun in my

purse. "And I have Kate, a highly competent woman who is addicted to exercise and self-defense courses."

Elizabeth looked unhappy. "Did these two men say *when* the murder would take place?"

"Christmas night, after everyone was exhausted and had had too much to drink. That gives us twenty-four hours to save a life, possibly my own."

I smiled, but Elizabeth did not.

"You must realize this is not the first time I've been threatened with bodily harm, nor I fear will it be the last. Two men attempted to kidnap me a decade after the poor Lindberg child was taken. My father subverted that one, and the men were apprehended. Then, when I was off at Radcliffe, I was accosted by a drunk Harvard lad who wouldn't take no for an answer. I handled that one with my knee to the appropriate part of his anatomy."

Elizabeth was staring at me wide-eyed.

"I could go on, but I won't," I said.

In reality, going on would have meant inventing more stories, and we didn't have time for that.

"Suffice it to say that when you are a woman with money and prestige, men often want you for their own nefarious purposes. It's one reason I've remained happily single all my life. Liaisons are quite enough for me—temporary and pleasurable."

"I really must take this to the general manager," she said, "and the police."

"You'll do no such thing. That will only drive our two would-be murderers underground."

Elizabeth looked stretched to her limit, and I took pity on her.

"Perhaps I've exaggerated the situation, and it was nothing more than idle talk. See what you can find out, my dear, about these two men—Joe Ryland and Mike Murch—and come to my suite at five this afternoon."

I pulled off one of my clip-on emerald earrings and handed it to her. No pierced ears for me. No pierced anything —what a barbaric idea.

"I'll leave this with you, and you may spread the word I've lost a valuable piece of jewelry. That will give you an excuse to visit me in case anyone is watching our interactions."

Elizabeth took the earring, put it in an envelope and stuffed it in the pocket of her concierge jacket.

"We'll put our heads together over a glass of wine this afternoon and decide what to do next," I said.

That's how we left it.

I had a few hours to kill—an unfortunate choice of words. I sidled through the lobby, pretending to take an interest in the fussy decorations. Every available space was draped in green-ery. I might as well have been on a cruise along the Amazon.

I entered the Flower Garden in time for tea, and I had to admit this was one part of the Palace Hotel that was exquis-itely decorated. Orchids were interspersed with poinsettias along the walls. Three Christmas trees were clustered in the center of the room.

I was seated immediately.

I looked around for Joe Ryland. Elizabeth had described him as a small, wiry man, always impeccably dressed. I saw such a man wandering near the periphery of the dining room and waved him over.

"Excuse me," I said, "but there seems to be a smudge on my water glass. Are you a waiter?"

"Joseph Ryland at your service. I'm a manager, but I can take care of that for you." He took the glass and motioned to my waiter to bring me another. "This is completely unaccept-able," he said to the waiter pointing to a spot that didn't exist. "You could lose your job over such carelessness."

"It's nothing," I said to the waiter. "Probably something I did when I took a sip."

The poor man nodded at me and disappeared. If I'd had any doubts about Joe Ryland, they were now erased. He was not a good man.

"Is there anything else I can do for you, Miss Wellington?" he asked.

"Ah, you know my name."

"Of course," he said. "You are one of our most distinguished guests."

"One of your oldest—is that what you meant?"

"Of course not."

Now I had Ryland on the defensive, right where I wanted him.

"Perhaps you *can* help me. It seems I've lost one of my earrings," I said, patting my ear. "Do you have a hotel detective or someone who might look for it? I'd offer a generous reward."

"I'll take care of it personally. Do you mind if I examine the other one?"

I handed it to him. "You may hold onto it for now. One earring is of little value."

"Yes, of course."

He licked his lips. To keep from drooling over it? I saw his eyes stray to my necklace.

"The necklace and earrings are part of a set, given to me by my father."

"Lovely," he said.

"People always say I should lock them away, but I say, what good is jewelry if you don't wear it? I keep it by my bedside at night. It's such a comfort to me, almost as if my father is still watching over me."

"Of course," Joe said. "You are quite sure the missing earring is not in your suite?"

"Quite sure."

"We'll locate it, I promise. If you don't mind I'll keep this, so the staff will know what to look for."

"Excellent." I was certain I wouldn't see that earring again until Joe and his co-conspirator Mike were arrested for my attempted murder.

I had that almost right.

I spent the next hours eating sweets I didn't want and drinking barely consumable tea. Tea bags, no less. I really should consider staying home next Christmas. I searched the dining room for single women like me—other wealthy old birds. I saw only two. One was considerably younger—in her late sixties I'd guess. And the other looked vaguely familiar. No harm in meeting them both.

I walked to the first woman and greeted her like a long lost friend.

"Oh, I apologize," I said. "You look so like my dear friend Elma. I'm sorry for interrupting your tea."

"You needn't apologize. It's a lovely tea, don't you think? Are you staying in the hotel?"

This led to a brief conversation. It seemed the woman in question had a husband who was out doing some last minute Christmas shopping.

The other woman was very much alone and someone I thought I knew from years past. She looked so old and drawn I thought perhaps I was mistaken. She, however, recognized me.

"Florence, is that you? What a surprise. Are you with anyone? Please join me."

I sat down but declined more tea. "Maude Merriwether. I haven't seen you, in what, ten years?"

"More like twenty."

"Are you also alone in the hotel this Christmas?" I asked.

"Very much so. My own decision. My granddaughter

invited me to stay with her, but frankly I felt like a quiet holiday this year. And you?"

"Same sentiment but no children or grandchildren."

"You never married, did you, Florence? I've often thought that was a wise decision. Connections so often bring heartache."

"I hope that's not a personal statement."

"My daughter died three years ago of cancer. I'm a religious person, so I know she's in a better place. My granddaughter, Leslie, is my last living relative. It was her new husband who insisted I come here. He's a dear man always looking out for my welfare and Leslie's. Leslie was left at the altar a year ago, and Jeffrey, her new husband, appeared as if by magic a few weeks later. They've been married six months. He's done so much for my Leslie—whisking her around the world, building her a lovely home on Long Island."

"So he's independently wealthy?" I asked.

"No, dear. I'm the one with the money. But what's the point of money except to bring happiness to others. All I had to do was supply the funds and he took care of the rest. I thought I was doing very well this year, but Jeffrey noticed I didn't seem happy. He suggested I could celebrate Christmas on my own terms without the bother of too many people around."

"I remember from our Radcliffe years that you loved Christmas as much as I did. We used to get into all kinds of mischief around the holidays."

"Quite true, but Jeffrey seemed to pick up on a sadness even I didn't recognize. He thought I wasn't done grieving for my daughter." Maude sighed. "I think perhaps he's right."

I studied Maude. She seemed so different from the last time I'd seen her. It was at a Radcliffe reunion, our fortieth perhaps. She was the life of the party, recently divorced but forging a new life. That's what she told me. She was surrounded by classmates, the way she'd always been in school. Everyone loved her, and everyone shared their secrets with her. Maude had this amazing ability to listen and never divulge what she heard.

"Why are you looking at me like that, Flo? Is my hair askew?" She patted her short white hair, well cut, and the Chanel suit that hugged her slim figure.

"No, you look just fine. I was thinking we should find some private time to catch up. If you don't have plans for Christmas, perhaps we could share a meal."

"I'd love that. I'm staying in room 462, the only thing they had available, but it's enough for one."

Room 462, the room where I heard the two men whispering. So Maude was their intended victim.

"I'm in the Royal Suite. My assistant, Kate, is staying with me, but we have plenty of space. Why don't you come Christmas Day and stay over?"

I was feeling desperate to protect Maude from whatever these two men had planned for her.

She looked at me oddly. "Dear Florence, you appear so intent on cheering me up. Has Leslie or Jeffrey been in touch with you?"

"No. Why?"

"They've seemed quite concerned about my mental state. Jeffrey suggested I see a psychiatrist he knew. He thought I might be depressed. Honestly, I felt worse after seeing the man, but the psychiatrist said that's what happened when one got in touch with hidden despair."

"Hidden despair?" I asked.

"Yes. Dr. Bacon said sometimes people didn't know how sad they really were. He gave me pills to sleep and podcasts to help me relax."

"You've always been the most relaxed and optimistic person I've ever known," I said.

"Hmm, I used to think that as well, but after a few sessions with him, I found myself feeling more and more hopeless. He used hypnosis on me and gave me sedatives for sleep, but nothing seemed to improve my mood. He agreed with my grandson's suggestion I spend Christmas in a luxury hotel and made me a special recording to use Christmas night. He said it was a difficult time for many people."

"This man sounds like a charlatan. Did you check out his credentials?"

"No. My grandson vouched for him, and I took his word on that. I think my family is genuinely concerned about me, afraid I might jump off a building or something. I'm not much fun these days, and I didn't want to dampen their holiday celebration. So staying away by myself sounded like a good idea."

She looked at me with an expression I'd never seen on her when we were in school. It was a look of resignation. "Young people don't understand that at some point life loses its luster. Has it done that for you, Flo?"

"No, I assure you it has not. I find a new adventure every day. Perhaps over the next twenty-four hours, you and I might even save a life."

Maude smiled. "You always had such a flair for the dramatic. I remember that from Radcliffe."

"How did you choose the Palace for your holiday?" I asked.

"Jeffrey knew one of the managers. He assured me the man would take good care of me—a Mike something."

I kept my face in a fixed smile. "Ah. Well. I'll expect to see you tomorrow afternoon around four. We'll make merry."

"I may not be good company, Flo."

"I shall be good enough company for both of us. I promise we'll have a lively time. By the way did you bring any jewelry on this trip?"

"What a strange question! You haven't become a jewel thief in your old age, have you? I really wouldn't put anything past you." She laughed—a lovely youthful musical sound.

"No. I just thought it might be fun to reminisce over old pieces. I know mine have stories to tell."

"You have become delightfully eccentric, Flo, but actually, I think you always were. I'll bring them with me tomorrow afternoon, if that's what you're suggesting, and we'll share our stories."

"Excellent."

I ARRIVED AT MY SUITE, thoroughly content with myself. I might be old but my brain seemed to be firing on all six cylinders. Or was it four these days? Whatever.

Kate met me at the door. "Where have you been? You said you'd be gone half an hour and it's been five hours, at least."

"You worry too much, Kate. It's not good for you at your age."

"I'm forty years old, half your age, so I think I can worry about you if I wish."

"People here believe I'm 90. I prefer the authority and maturity those extra years give me—not to mention the shock on people's faces to see me mobile and alert."

"You're incorrigible," Kate said.

"I need something to drink," I said.

"Tea?"

"I've had enough bad tea to last me a lifetime. I want something stronger, and then we need to talk."

While Kate and I savored a lovely Speyside single malt, I told her what I was up to. She did not interrupt once. Kate remained in my employ because she knew never to interrupt me and rarely to give me advice.

Elizabeth knocked on the door when I'd finished. Kate invited her in, and they exchanged a hug.

"You look wonderful," Kate said.

"As do you," Elizabeth responded.

"Enough chitchat. You're precisely on time," I said. "I like that. Scotch?"

"Unfortunately, I'm still on duty."

"Are you working tomorrow?" I asked.

"I am, a double shift, filling in for people who want to spend Christmas with their families. I'm Buddhist, so Christmas is just another day for me." She looked at my expectant face. "I do have information about Mr. Ryland and Mr. Murch."

"That would be Joe and Mike—the men I told you about, Kate."

"They are both relatively new hires, within the last six months."

"I see. And have there been any robberies within that period of time?" I asked.

"Yes. One older woman lost a brooch and another a ring. Management was quick to make amends, and neither woman filed a complaint. A member of the housekeeping staff was fired, but I knew the woman. She was an honest worker."

"No . . how shall I put it . . . no untimely deaths?"

"Nothing of that sort, I'm glad to say, Miss Wellington. Are you certain you heard the conversation clearly?"

"Despite my age, my hearing has remained acute. I heard what I told you."

"I meant no offense. I just thought we should be very certain about the current risk. If, as you say, your life is being threatened, I really must report this to the General Manager and notify the police."

I sighed heavily. "I have a far better plan."

Elizabeth and Kate were silent as I spoke.

"I'm quite sure the real target is Maude Merriwether. She's alone and far more vulnerable than I. She'll be joining us tomorrow with her jewelry and staying over. It's the only way I could think to protect her. Your job, Elizabeth, will be to let that information be known once I have Maude safely in the suite, say around five or so."

Elizabeth shook her head. "This is a terrible idea."

Kate put a hand on her arm. "Flo hired me fifteen years ago after she saw me in the Olympics biathlon. I'm an excellent shot obviously, and I've stayed in training since then. Both women will be safe here."

"I'll be happy to have the police on speed dial," I said, "once we catch our crooks. But they must not be involved before then. If you call them in, nothing will happen."

Elizabeth left without making eye contact.

Kate and I slept soundly that night and celebrated Christmas the next morning with mimosas and eggs Benedict. We opened handmade Christmas stockings, something Kate had purchased at a Vienna Christmas fair years ago and something we filled for one another with trinkets each Christmas. She'd had our names embroidered on them. That touched me deeply although I didn't let her know that. Too sentimental.

How I got through Christmas day until Maude arrived I'm sure I don't know. I went to the Fitness Center for an hour, took a long bath with bath salts Kate had ordered from France, wandered the lobby of the hotel which was bustling with families eager for brunch in the Flower Garden, and gave Maude a call to make sure she was still coming at four.

"Of course, Florence, I'm looking forward to it."

I passed by the lobby on my way to the elevators and noticed Elizabeth chatting with Joe Ryland at the front desk. They looked a little too cozy for my liking. Elizabeth was not always the best judge of men—that's where Kate had come in years ago. She and I got her away from a very unsavory sort before he could harm her in any lasting way.

A long story and a long time ago, but I wondered now if Elizabeth was the woman I thought she was. She grinned and laughed with Joe Ryland, a greasy little character if ever there was one. What if she'd told Ryland about my suspicions?

They stopped talking as I walked past—both smiled in my direction.

I entered the apartment and headed straight for the piano. I started with Bach and moved on to Beethoven.

"You sound like you're pounding on that poor piano, not playing it," Kate said.

"I am disturbed if you must know. I saw Elizabeth chatting it up with Joe Ryland. They were laughing. If she told him what I suspected, then our plans are ruined."

"You don't trust many people, do you Flo?" Kate said.

"No. A secret is a secret only as long as it is told to no one."

"Well, I trust Elizabeth," Kate said. "She learned her lesson about men."

"I hope you're right, but you must admit she thinks I'm an eccentric, not to be fully believed."

"You *are* an eccentric, Flo," Kate said.

I continued playing the piano until Kate begged me to stop. Then I sat, twiddling my thumbs.

"Can't you read a book?" Kate asked. "I have an exceptionally good thriller I've just finished."

"I'm not into fiction," I said, "and don't shake your head again—I'm quite tired of that behavior."

"Curmudgeon," Kate said, but she held her head steady. She knew which side her bread was buttered on.

The clock on the mantle chimed four. Maude arrived five minutes later with a lovely brocade overnight bag in one hand and a wrapped present in the other.

"Oh, dear," I said. "I didn't think of getting you a present."

"Lifting my spirits is present enough," Maude said pleasantly. "But the gift isn't for you, it's for Kate. I'm sure she didn't bargain on a third person in this suite, so this is a thank-you gift."

"It's a delight to have you, Mrs. Merriwether," Kate said. "You'll have the room next to Miss Wellington, and I will have the adjoining room on the other side of you. All very snug."

"Please, you must call me Maude." With that she handed Kate an elegantly wrapped package. "I took the liberty of asking in the shop downstairs if they knew you and what size you might wear."

Kate opened the present. Inside was a light white jacket. "Perfect to wear to my workouts," Kate said. "Thank you."

Did I feel a ping of jealousy? I'd never bought Kate clothes, nor had I the least idea what size she might be. They looked quite chummy standing there—Maude and Kate, and Maude could never be accused of being a curmudgeon.

I clapped my hands. "Enough of this. Let's get on with our plans."

We ordered room service and discussed what the evening might bring. Maude was silent until I reached the part about Mike Murch.

"He came to my room earlier this afternoon," she said. "He seemed like a charming young man, and he said he knew my grandson."

"Your grandson-in-law," I corrected.

"Yes, but really, Flo, I simply can't believe Mr. Murch would mean to harm me. He seemed very interested in my well-being and my plans for tonight. He said he was delighted I would not be alone."

"I'm afraid, Maude, you have always been too trusting. Mike Murch was supposed to come on duty at eight pm, so what was he doing at your room this afternoon?"

Maude looked miffed. "You've always been a suspicious person."

"And you were not suspicious of your husband's secretary," I said. "That led to your divorce, I believe."

Even *I* knew that was a low blow.

Maude looked stricken.

Suddenly, I felt another unpleasant feeling—shame perhaps.

"Apologize," Kate said under her breath. "Now."

I hesitated. Apologizing was not in my repertoire. But Maude did look upset, and she'd come to us hoping to be cheered up.

"I'm sorry, Maude. I'm used to speaking my mind. I've lived alone too long."

Maude turned to me. "What you said is true. I am gullible. People sometimes take advantage of me."

"And I have always been too cynical," I said. "People steer clear of me."

It was a fact, but I wasn't sure I minded it.

After dinner, Kate made quite a show of leaving to visit her family, proclaiming loudly in the lobby she wouldn't be returning until the following night. She even asked someone to order her a cab. We waved goodbye to her as she headed out.

Elizabeth had told Kate the best reentry route. She was to pass through the kitchen wearing a food service uniform. If anyone stopped her, she was to say she was hired for the holidays and provide the badge Elizabeth made for her. She was unlikely to encounter Joe or Mike as they never entered the kitchen, but just in case she would wear a wig and glasses.

That part went smoothly. At nine pm Kate knocked on our door and offered us a Buche de Noël, which she said we'd ordered. If anyone had heard us talking in the hall, it would seem completely authentic. We ushered her inside and hoped no one would notice she never exited the suite.

For an hour, we sat by the fire, ate our Buche de Noël, and drank the strongest coffee we could find. We gave Maude a glass of brandy instead and explained that if she went to sleep that would be all the better. She didn't object to that idea, and she also didn't seem particularly afraid of what might happen.

"Don't you remember, Flo, all those pranks you pulled at school? Don't you recall how eager I was to go along with you?'

I nodded slowly. I'd always thought I'd pulled off those escapades on my own. But in reality, I hadn't. Maude had been at my side. She was an easy person to underestimate.

"I'd forgotten that, Maude. You never said no to any of my schemes as long as they didn't hurt another person. Of course, the worry here, is that you might be the person harmed."

"I doubt that. I have complete faith in you and Kate."

We dimmed the lights shortly after ten and went to our respective rooms. We locked our doors but not the ones that connected our bedrooms. It was obvious Mike and Joe would have master keys, and I didn't want anything to seem amiss.

For a long while everything was quiet. I found myself drifting off and shifted to a chair where I tried to read one of the books Kate had given me.

What I never expected was that Maude might leave of her own accord, but that is precisely what happened at midnight.

Kate and I both heard a door between us open and close. We charged into Maude's room only to discover it empty. Her bathroom door was closed. We assumed that's where she was.

We waited a minute and then called out to her. No answer. Kate opened the bathroom door and found the room empty.

By the time we made it to the foyer, she was gone, and the massive front door to the suite was closed.

The hallway outside was quiet and there was no evidence of a struggle. The lights were low—no one ever took my complaints seriously—so it was hard to see anything beyond a few feet.

"Does your friend sleepwalk?" Kate asked.

"I wouldn't know," I said. "She's really more of an acquaintance."

Kate gave me a look. "Whatever you wish to call her, she's gone. You have your derringer?"

"Of course," I said.

"And your cell phone?"

"What do you take me for? I have my gun, my cell phone, and I'm wearing my workout shoes. Stop wasting time."

"We'll split up, but text me your location every five minutes," Kate said. "I'll do the same."

I headed left. Kate went right.

I walked a few feet, listened, heard nothing, and moved on. I glanced back at Kate before we both turned down separate corridors.

Nothing. No sounds. No movement. The dim lighting made me see shadows everywhere, but they were only that. Had Maude gone to the lobby for some reason?

If so, she'd be safe. At least I hoped so. There was always someone at the desk or should be. Then, I remembered how easy it had been for me to snoop around the front desk with the clerk sleeping in the back. What if Mike Murch was the only person awake or perhaps the only one on duty?

I texted Elizabeth to let her know that Maude had disappeared, but I got no reply. That worried me. Perhaps I was right about Elizabeth—maybe she didn't believe me or even worse perhaps she was in cahoots with the two men. Why else would she fail to call me back?

Then I texted Kate. "See anything?"

"Nothing," she wrote back.

I'd come to the end of the corridor and approached the circular marble staircase that led down to the lobby. When Kate didn't care to go to the Fitness Center, she loved to run up and down those stairs. She always wanted me to come with her, but running up and down stairs seemed ridiculous to me— an older woman in a tracksuit. What a complete lack of decorum.

I peered over the banister of the spiral staircase into a void. Anyone who fell from this height would be killed instantly when they landed on the marbled mezzanine five floors beneath me. I felt a touch of vertigo as I peered over the edge and had to straighten up to get my bearings. With both hands on the mahogany bannister, I looked again. I thought I saw some movement one flight below me. I squinted. Was a person leaning over the banister?

I texted Kate. Then, I ran down the flight of stairs and slowed as I saw Maude swaying slightly a few feet beneath me. She was standing on tiptoe, lifting one leg as if she meant to climb over the railing. It was likely she'd tumble head first to the mezzanine before she managed to get her leg over the bannister.

I called softly to her, and she turned her head toward me. Her eyes were closed, and she had a sickeningly serene smile on her lips. Was she asleep? She seemed to be listening to something, nodding slightly. I saw her ear buds and heard a whisper, more like a hiss. One ear bud was in, the other out.

There was no time to wait for Kate. I crept to her, grabbed her waist and yanked her safely back onto the staircase. We both fell with a thud onto the marble tread. Maude barely reacted, opening her eyes and smiling at me as if she were drunk.

"Almost over," she whispered. "You've come to join me? We could fly together to eternity."

I held her tight and shushed her. Then I listened to the recording on her iPhone. It was a man's voice, soft, soothing.

"Feel the euphoria, Maude. Deep sleep and weightlessness. Climb over to the other side. Look up. See the sky? Let go. Fly to the sky."

Kate appeared, and together we took the semiconscious Maude to our rooms. We sat her on the sofa, rubbed her hands, and used my smelling salts to rouse her. Nothing works quite as effectively as smelling salts to jolt a person into consciousness.

Her eyes flew open. "What are you doing to me? Are you trying to kill me?"

"Save you," I said. As she came round, we settled her back on the couch and gathered pillows to support her.

"Save me? From what? I was having the most delightful dream. Everything was going to be all right."

Kate brought her a cup of coffee. I sat with Maude as she drank it, while Kate checked the apartment.

Very little had been disturbed except for the safe in the dining room which had been opened. So someone had been in our rooms, but we'd put none of our jewelry in the safe. They were in a false bottom of Kate's suitcase tucked in the back of her closet.

"Everything is fine," Kate said.

"Not fine at all, we didn't catch our thieves," I said.

Someone knocked on the outer door and then Elizabeth burst through it before we could answer. Two of Boston's finest were with her. "Thank goodness," she said when she found us together on the sofa. "You're all right then?"

We nodded.

"Why didn't you call me back?" I asked.

"No time. I had to get the police—we ran upstairs and saw Joe and Mike leaving your suite. They said they'd come at your request and left when they saw the suite was empty." Elizabeth paused to catch her breath. "Then when we couldn't find you—well, I thought the worst might have happened. Thank God you're all right. We've got Mr. Ryland and Mr. Murch in custody downstairs. Tell us what happened."

Bit by bit Maude told her story. Kate and I finished with the final details.

"You found nothing on them?" I asked.

"Joe had your necklace. He claimed you'd asked him to keep it in the downstairs safe when you'd called him to come to your room," Elizabeth said. "But, of course, I knew you'd never called him."

"I left that necklace out where he couldn't resist taking it. All the rest of the jewelry is safe in the bottom of Kate's suitcase."

"Good," Elizabeth said. "Mostly I'm simply relieved you're safe. If anything had happened to you, I couldn't have lived with myself. That's why I contacted the police earlier today. Your scheme was too risky."

"Yes, yes," I said. "Thank you, Elizabeth, for disobeying me about the police."

"My pleasure."

Once Maude started talking it didn't seem she could stop. We'd heard some of it before, but the detective who came to interview us wrote copious notes.

"I can't believe Jeffrey is involved with this. He's only expressed concern for me and Leslie."

"Who stands to inherit if anything happens to you?" I asked.

"Leslie is my sole heir. If she were to die then Jeffrey would inherit everything. You're suggesting he meant to get rid of me and then Leslie? That can't be."

"Did you do a background check on him when Leslie decided to marry him?" Kate asked.

"No. That seemed vulgar. I was simply glad Leslie had found happiness." Maude put her face in her hands. "How can you be sure he was involved?"

"He's the one who suggested the psychiatrist Dr. Bacon," I said, "if he even is a psychiatrist—which I doubt. And Bacon was the man who made the podcast, gave you sedatives, convinced you that you were depressed."

"The sedatives left me feeling groggy, in a fog," Maude said. "I met with the doctor weekly and didn't feel any better. He said that many people got depressed during the holidays."

"But you always loved Christmas," I said.

"You're right, I couldn't understand it myself. Dr. Bacon said feelings change as people get older—what they once loved they might come to hate. He suggested hypnosis and said he'd make a special recording for me, like a podcast, to be used Christmas night but not before. He and Jeffrey thought I should get away from the stress of the holiday season.

"Jeffrey arranged everything. I came here, not because I wanted to but because I felt I would be a bother to the family at a time when they wanted a happy Christmas."

Maude stopped talking and looked miserable. "I've caused so much trouble. Maybe you should have let me go, Flo."

"Nonsense. You exposed Jeffrey for what he is and saved your granddaughter from a lifetime of misery. You should be very proud of yourself."

"It will break my Leslie's heart," Maude said.

"Her heart will mend," I said. "Saving her life is what matters."

"You're right, Flo," Maude said. "I've always been an optimistic person, even when my husband left me. I couldn't understand what was happening to me. The more I saw the doctor, the worse I felt. Even Leslie seemed upset and concerned about me."

Kate took Maude's hand. "You've been through a lot, but you're safe now."

"I'm so grateful to both of you," Maude said. "How lucky I was to find you here, Flo."

It was difficult for me to say what came next. "I'm glad you wandered back into my life. I could use a friend my own age, and perhaps your optimism will be contagious."

"Amen to that," Kate said.

I gave her a sharp look, but Kate met my gaze. "You did good," she said and squeezed my hand.

Maude, Kate, and I went downstairs with the police officers to sign a formal statement.

On the way, I took a moment to talk with Elizabeth. "I doubted you, and I'm sorry about that. When I saw you talking to Joe Ryland, I didn't know what to think."

"He'd seen me leave your room, so I had to come up with some explanation. I told him you were unhappy about the decorations in the suite because there weren't any, and we laughed about that. I can see how you misinterpreted what you saw."

"And I can see why you are such a wonderful concierge— always calm and ever the diplomat."

"I couldn't go along with your request for no police. That was too dangerous, but I kept them out of sight until I needed them."

We found Joe and Mike in the lobby handcuffed in a back office waiting to be removed to the city jail.

I edged close to them as Maude and Kate stood near the front desk reviewing their statements.

It didn't take much to get the two men bickering. I spoke quietly and simply mentioned the number of years they would each get for attempted murder and robbery. My obsession with *Law and Order* reruns was helpful that night. I suggested they turn state's evidence and identify the real culprit.

Mike Murch started shouting. "It wasn't my idea. I don't kill people. It's her grandson—Jeffrey Jones. He's the one."

"Shut up," Ryland said.

The officer in charge came over. I tried to look innocent and stepped out of his way. He read them their rights and then asked if either of them wished to make a statement.

"I do," Mike said. "You shut up if you want. You wait for your lawyer, but I'm not involved in a charge of attempted murder. Ryland and Jones are cousins. Jones promised us

Maude would kill herself, and all Ryland and I had to do was gather up her jewelry."

"You idiot," Ryland yelled. "Look what you've done."

"He's probably saved you from a charge of attempted murder," I said.

The officer shot me a look.

"Sorry," I said.

Of course, I wasn't.

Mike wasn't either. "I don't want anything to do with these creeps. Yeah, I was willing to fence some stolen jewelry. I admit that. But I'm not a violent man. Don't own a gun. I'll tell you everything you want to know about Ryland and Jones if you give me a break."

The officer waved over two other police to take the men away. We stayed in the lobby while our suite was being examined by crime scene experts. While we waited, Maude got a call from her granddaughter, Leslie. I was sitting next to her and I could hear how distraught Leslie sounded.

"Are you all right? The police just picked up Jeffrey."

After Maude assured her she was fine, Leslie acknowledged she'd begun to suspect Jeffrey was more interested in her money than in her.

She insisted on coming over. When she arrived hours later, we were back upstairs. We went over everything once more. Maude seemed to relish retelling her story. Leslie looked more and more upset.

"I could have gotten you killed. All of you killed," she said.

"Nonsense," Maude said. "I was well protected. Flo and Kate knew precisely what to do. Frankly, my dear, it was all rather exciting. I know for you it's dreadful, but now it's over, and we're all safe."

I took a close look at Maude. Her blue eyes sparkled and she had color in her cheeks. She looked exactly like the young woman I knew from Radcliffe after we'd had a successful escapade together.

She giggled. "Life hasn't been nearly as much fun since we lost touch years ago, Flo."

I had to agree.

All's well that ends well.

Actually, for Maude and me, it was more of a beginning. She was in need of adventures and I was in need of a friend. We had the money to do precisely what we wanted, whether that was travel, serve as undercover hotel critics, or solve crimes. Kate was happy to be our sidekick.

As it turned out, murder—preventing it that is—proved to be our forte. After all, how much can you actually fear in your eighties? We'd already had a good run, and more was simply gravy.

THE END

2

A CURMUDGEON'S LAST CHRISTMAS

"Hurry. Don't just stand there like two door stoppers. Come in here!" I didn't mean to yell, but sometimes one had to be more forceful than one might like. "Three days to Christmas, and we have a life to save. The Grim Reaper is standing at the poor man's door."

Kate stared at me. "Most people mellow with age, Flo. You seem to be headed in the other direction—you wake us up at five in the morning, ask us to pack our bags, and expect us in your office at six."

"So? It's literally one flight down from your bedrooms. What else are you doing? I can answer that. Nothing."

Kate rolled her eyes. She was forty years old and acting like a schoolgirl.

"What, Kate, I didn't give you time for your workout this morning?"

"No, you didn't as a matter of fact, but I'm more

concerned about Maude. You promise her a relaxing Christmas vacation and then you haul her out of bed on her first morning here. It's not the least bit gracious."

She had a point. I stared out the window at the dusting of snow over the Boston Public Garden. My neighboring brownstones glistened while the white flakes continued to fall. It was a lovely sight.

But it wasn't one we had time for.

"When have you ever considered me a gracious person, Kate? And is Maude complaining?"

Kate sighed heavily. "Maude never complains, and I suppose the answer to your first question is also never."

"Fine, then. That's settled. Get in here. I've cleared off the desk, so you can see the map of where we're headed."

Kate shook her head. "You cleared off your desk by dumping everything on the floor."

"So what? Natalie comes every day, whisks her little duster around the rooms. She can add this to her minimal duties."

"You are impossible," Kate said.

"Sometimes you act as if you haven't known me for fifteen years," I said. "I am entirely predictable."

"Yes. And unlikely to change."

"Quite. Now, Maude, I haven't heard a peep from you. Are you awake?"

"Almost. I'm not quite as young as you are, so it takes me a bit of time to get going."

"What, you're six months older than me if that. Eighty one on your next birthday?"

"Eighty-two."

"But we were in the same class at Radcliffe," I said.

"You skipped your last year in finishing school," Maude said. "You can't have forgotten that. It's all you talked about when you arrived."

"You're right. I had to get away from the stupidity of that

so-called school. I still have to work on keeping my pinky down when I drink tea."

Maude smiled, but she did look tired, as if she might have benefited from another couple hours of sleep.

"Very well, you're a year older than I am. Take a chair if you like."

Kate pulled over a well-worn Gainsborough, but Maude declined.

"I'm fine," she said, "and I'd like to see clearly where we're headed."

I smoothed out an Esso Road Map of Cape Cod across the top of my father's partner desk—not that I'd ever allow a partner to sit there with me. The map covered most of the leather surface.

"This map is ancient," Kate said. "It's probably older than you are."

"If it was good enough for my father's chauffeur, it's good enough for me."

"You can't even read the town names in the creases," she persisted.

"That's enough. There is only one difficult person allowed in this house, and as you have repeatedly said, that person is me."

I smiled.

"Actually," I said, "our mission is to save another curmudgeon from harm. A man who lives on Cape Cod . . . just there." I pointed to a spot near Falmouth. As Kate had indicated, I could only read the letters FAL before the rest disappeared into a fold that would soon become a tear if I wasn't careful.

Kate and Maude leaned over to see where my finger rested.

"I had a boyfriend in West Falmouth," Kate said. "That looks to be where we're headed."

"Yes. West Falmouth," I said.

"I haven't been there in years," Kate said. "This could be fun. I wonder if I should give Jimmy a call. No, maybe not. We didn't part on the best of terms."

"We are not making a social visit, Kate. We'll be working. I have an acquaintance in West Falmouth, and she seems especially concerned about a certain gentleman. He's not a popular fellow according to Jayne, and lately, he's had a series of 'accidents'. She's afraid that someone may wish to do him in."

"My, my," Maude said, "we *are* needed."

"Precisely. I'm not sure how she knew to call me."

"You don't think it had to do with the article in the Boston Globe that you made me share on your Facebook page?" Kate asked. "Or the business cards you want me to pass around like Christmas candy?"

"Perhaps."

"I have to admit the reporter wrote a first-rate article," Kate said. "'Grand Dame from Boston's Elite Saves Friend from Murder.' It read like a short story. I wouldn't have believed it if I hadn't been there."

"Nor would I," Maude said. "I do love our business cards." She took one out of her card case and rubbed her hand along the gold-embossed names at the top. "I never thought I'd see my name on a business card: Wellington and Merriwether. Your name should be here as well, Kate."

"I'm happy to fly under the radar," Kate said, "the power behind the throne and all that."

It was a feeble attempt to get a rise out of me and it failed. Of course I knew Kate was the brawn behind our brains, and sometimes had a useful mind of her own. But there was no need to inflate her ego. She had quite enough self-confidence already.

"The cards make a statement, don't they," I said, "that we are financially secure and that clients should expect to pay dearly for our priceless services."

"Unless, of course, they are people you know or people who really need our help," Kate said. "How much money have you actually made on this venture?"

"Some money from Maude," I said, "She insisted on paying us, but she's the only one. Still, you mustn't forget we're a start-up."

" 'ODPA: Old Dames Protection Agency' is a nice touch," Maude said, running her fingers along the bottom of the card. "I'm proud of that—it makes it clear we're not apologizing for our age."

Kate couldn't remain silent. "As I've already said, it might be more accurate to call yourselves 'OODPA,' Odd Old Dames Protection Agency. No offense, Maude."

"None taken, dear. Flo has always been eccentric, and I have always been too stuck in my ways. She's showing me a whole new side of life, and I like it."

"Bravo," I said. "Now, may we get back to work?" I didn't wait for an answer. "We'll stay in a summer home that my friend knows is available. It's very near the water and the home of our potential murder victim." I handed Kate the address. "I'm sure you can find this with your ESP."

"GPS," Kate said.

"Close enough. Just get us there. I said we'd meet Jayne at noon for lunch at a little restaurant she knows about—Dana's Kitchen."

"Dana's Kitchen! That's where Jimmy and I would have lunch after we biked along the Shining Sea Path," Kate said.

"Please, Kate, focus. We are not taking a bicycle trip down memory lane. We're trying to save a man's life."

THE TRIP to Cape Cod was quick. Kate had made me add another car—a BMW and my first SUV. She said if we were going to drive all over the country preventing crime, we should do it in comfort and style with The Ultimate Driving Machine. Not that I drove us anywhere—Kate was our designated driver.

She got us to West Falmouth in under ninety minutes, hours before our lunch date. The house key lay under the doormat of a pleasant, unfussy home that had a lovely view of the water. We chose our bedrooms, dropped off our luggage, and then toured the village. Jayne had given us addresses for the curmudgeon's house and his shoe repair shop located near the West Falmouth Market.

We started with his house located on Blacksmith Shop Road near an old Quaker cemetery. From Jayne's description of the man, I wondered if the dead Quakers were twitching in their graves at the thought of this nasty individual living among them. I found the idea so amusing I shared it with my entourage.

Kate just shook her head, but Maude responded.

"Quakers have a lot of their own stories to tell," she said. "Not as picture perfect as you might believe. Although some are," she added quickly.

"Maude, it's all right to speak ill of the dead," I said. "We just don't want to add one more to that list. Here's the house on the left. Slow down, Kate. There he is!"

In front of a house in need of care stood a sixty-year old man, looking only slightly less bedraggled than the house behind him. He was wearing worn-out overalls and had a scrappy dog beside him, doing his business. Both glared at us as we drove by.

"Stop, Kate, and I'll have a word."

She parked across the street a short distance up from the house.

The man barely let me get out of the car before he began

bellowing. "Who the hell are you? What are you doing driving along a private road in your fancy-schmancy car?"

"Hello, sir. My name is Florence Wellington, and I've come to look at a house for sale on this road."

"Well, it sure as hell ain't mine! Stay away." He put his hand out as if he were a traffic guard telling me to stop. "I got my rifle inside the house. Get off my property."

Kate started to climb out of the car. I had no doubt she had her revolver close at hand, but the last thing I wanted was to escalate the situation. I motioned her back inside.

I stopped near the edge of his property and pretended to look at his mailbox for a name. "Mr. Sanford, is it? That's an old Quaker name. Have you lived here long? I came to Cape Cod with my parents every summer as a child, and I have such a longing to be back here."

I used every trick I could think of to warm this man's heart. It worked only a little.

"We don't want interlopers of any kind," he said. "The house you're looking for is at the foot of the road—can't see how you missed it with its big gaudy sign."

"I'm so sorry," I said. Kate must have been proud—I actually sounded sorry. "We're staying at a house near West Falmouth Harbor, but as a child we stayed in one of the houses on this road. I just can't remember which one."

"That was a long time ago," the man said, "from the look of you."

I smiled sweetly or as close as I could come to sweet. "Yes, eons ago."

"It was probably the big house up the hill," the man said. "It's the only house big enough for people like you—folks with too much money. But I don't want you anywhere near that place."

"All I'd like to do is look at it. See if it is the one I visited as a child. We'll just walk up the road and take a quick look around—if you don't mind."

"I do mind. That house is privately owned. Stay off that property and mine as well. Ain't nothing for sale up this way."

"As you wish. We'll need to drive up this road in order to turn around—our car's too big to maneuver it here."

Mr. Sanford grunted a reply and took his dog inside.

Kate drove us to the top of the hill and around a half circle near what looked like an abandoned house. I asked her to stop.

"Mr. Sanford seemed very anxious to keep us away from this place. I wonder why."

It was a lovely old home but one that had seen better days. It bordered on the Quaker graveyard and appeared to be deserted. I tried several doors, all locked. A sign near the front door ordered us to stay out, that anyone entering the house would be prosecuted. Kate looked at me, and I nodded.

First, she casually knocked over the sign and covered it with a few remaining leaves from the fall. Then she jimmied the lock on the front door, and in moments we were inside. A few sticks of furniture were all that remained in the entrance hall and in the front and back parlor. It wasn't as dusty as I expected, but it was colder than I might have hoped. Maude was shivering. She was a thin woman, and even I, with my substantial bulk, found it quite miserable.

Kate ran to the car and brought us back scarves and mittens to add to our winter coats. We headed to the kitchen in the back with no real hope of salvation, but that's where everything changed. The kitchen was warm. A large fireplace smelled of smoke. Next to it lay a neatly stacked pile of wood.

Kate flicked a light switch, and the overhead light in the kitchen came on. "Electricity," she said. "Why would there be electricity? Someone is obviously living here. Look."

Off to the side of the kitchen where there was space for a

table lay a mattress, covered in quilts and big enough for two people. A space heater stood nearby.

The kitchen itself had been swept clean.

Kate called out, "Is anyone here?"

There was no answer.

"Upstairs," Kate said. She took her revolver out of her coat pocket. "Squatters, I imagine, but that wouldn't explain why the electricity was on. I wonder who's paying that bill."

We followed Kate up the stairs to three empty bedrooms. The space got colder and colder as we moved farther from the kitchen. In the third bedroom, a rustling sound made us jump.

"Rats," Kate said. She turned on the light and we heard a scramble, then a sharp little cry. Someone scooted past us, down the stairs and out the front door.

"What in the world was that?" Maude asked. "It was human, wasn't it?"

"Human, all right," Kate said. "But I can't say much more than that. Someone wearing a parka, hat and gloves, intent on staying warm I'd guess—or well-disguised. But I don't know if it was man or woman, adult or child. Did you see anything else, Flo?"

I so wanted to make some profound announcement. After all, I was head of ODPA, but actually I'd seen less than Kate. More like a flash. "Small, young, I would guess. Agile. He or she was gone before we knew it."

"Yes," Kate said. "I think that creature could have outrun me."

That was a statement. Kate was a devotee of cross-training and running marathons. While she wasn't at her peak the way she was in her Olympic biathlon days, she wasn't far from it.

Maude had been poking around the room as we talked. "Look," she said, picking up a scrap of material. It was a red and green plaid flannel, a small triangle, neatly cut as if it was meant to be used for something.

"It looks as if it's a piece for a quilt," Maude said.

"A really curious clue," I said. "Are there more of these little pieces lying around?"

We searched the area carefully, and Maude found the prize tucked away at the back of the small closet: a man's cotton shirt missing a sleeve, a pair of scissors beside it.

"Whoa," I said. "So was that munchkin we saw a woman working on a quilt of some sort in a freezing closet?"

We found nothing more.

"To the kitchen," Kate said. "I'll start a fire, and we'll see where we are."

We followed her down the stairs. I flipped on the heater and stood beside it warming my hands as Kate built the fire.

Maude shook her head when I motioned her over. "I'm fine. Look at all the food on the counter. Someone means to live here for a while."

I joined her and found mulling spices and apple cider. "Okay, this is strange," I said. "Squatters with a sense of the finer things in life. A touch of Christmas."

I examined the stove. "It's electric. Hot cider would warm us up nicely."

Maude looked at me aghast. "We can't steal someone's food," she said. "We've already broken and entered."

"We won't use much of it and we'll leave money. You don't see any rum lying around, do you Maude?"

"No."

"Just as well, I suppose. We need to keep our wits about us."

The fire blazed. The mulled apple cider gave off its delectable scent, and for a moment even I thought all was right with the world.

Of course, that wasn't about to last.

We heard a car roar up the driveway to the house. No sirens to tell us what was going on. Then a lot of pounding.

"Police! Open up!'

Kate put her revolver back in her zippered inside pocket and walked ahead of us to the front door.

"We're coming," she shouted. "We are unarmed."

Kate opened the door, and two uniformed police entered, guns drawn.

"It's two old ladies, Walt," the first one said. "Put your gun away."

"What about this one?" Walt asked, pointing at Kate. "Want me to pat her down?"

"That won't be necessary. You packing, miss?"

Kate hesitated. "I always carry a small gun for protection. I have a license."

"I'll be damned," the officer said. "Where's your license?"

"Back pocket."

"Turn around nice and slow."

Kate followed his direction.

"Okay, pull it out."

She handed it to him. He looked it over and handed it back. "It's in order. Now, what are you doing here? A man down the road saw smoke from the chimney and called us to investigate. This house has been empty for years."

"Was the man Mr. Sanford?" I asked.

"Yeah, he's the one. You know him?"

"We met him," I said. "We'd come to look at this house— it's a house I thought I'd stayed in as a child. We were all freezing, and the door was wide open, so we walked inside."

It was a tiny lie, more of an exaggeration, really.

"We found wood stacked for a fire and food on the counter, so we stayed to warm up. Someone has been living here from the look of things."

"I need to call this in," the first officer said, "and I'll need to see your IDs. How long have you been here?"

"About half an hour," Kate said. "Someone else was here

when we entered, hiding out upstairs. The person ran out when we discovered them."

"Description?"

"Small, covered up in a parka, hat. We couldn't see much of anything about him or her."

"Hmm," the officer said. "That's convenient. A mysterious person disappears when you enter."

"Look, officer"—I glanced at his name tag—"Officer Dunlap. You can ask Mr. Sanford—he talked with us half an hour ago. He'll know we haven't been hanging around the house."

"Good idea. Let's go."

We drove slowly down the hill, following the police car. If I'd thought Mr. Sanford was unhappy to see us earlier, that was nothing compared to now.

"You found the culprits, Dudley?" he yelled from inside the screen door of his house.

"It's Dunlap, as you well know, John. These women say they talked to you earlier?"

"What?" John roused himself enough to step outside with his dog and his rifle beside him.

"No need for the gun, John," Officer Dunlap said. "You called 911 to have us check out the big house."

"So I did. That doesn't mean I talked to these women earlier. I've never seen these women in my life." John Sanford continued his tirade. "They're up to no good—that's for sure. I want everyone off my property, including you so-called police-men. Where were you when I needed you this month? I told you someone was out to finish me off, and you think it's a joke."

"We come when you call, John. That's our job."

"You come and you do a big fat nothing."

There was a long moment of silence during which I did some quick thinking.

"Mr. Sanford, I talked to you this morning under false pretenses. I'm not looking for a house to buy. I believe you have a friend Jayne Winston. She thinks you are in danger, as you say you are. She hired us to protect you."

Every male mouth fell open.

"Jayne Winston hired two old birds and a young one to keep me from getting murdered?"

"Exactly," I said.

"I thought she was a friend. She nursed my dog back to health, and I owe her for that. But now this? She's turned on me, too."

"No, she hasn't, Mr. Sanford. Perhaps you've read about us in the Boston Globe—Jayne had. I'm head of an organization called ODPA. We prevent murders from happening." I handed him a card.

Mr. Sanford leaned against the door frame. "ODPA. Jayne read me an article about you. My eyesight's going, so she reads me the paper once a week—just the good bits. We shared a laugh about you—Old Dames Protection Agency—and then we read what you done over the last year. That's when Jayne stopped laughing."

"I've known Jayne for years," I said. "I contribute to her Cape Cod animal shelter, and that's where we met. She's very persuasive. She almost convinced me I needed a Great Dane as a companion in my old age. I assured her I already had a companion—Kate here."

"Thanks a lot," Kate said.

"In any case, we remained friends. I told her to call me any time she needed help, and now she has."

"Humph," was all John Sanford could manage, but I could tell by the way he looked at me, he thought I might just be telling the truth.

He nodded at the officers. "You can go, Dudley. I did talk

to this woman, but I told her not to go to that house on the hill."

Officer Dunlap nodded. "You should know squatters appear to be living in the house. We'll keep an eye on it."

"The same way you kept an eye on things when I was nearly shot in the woods or the time I almost lost my leg in a steel bear trap. Or maybe after I got accidentally poisoned by a bad piece of meat."

"Look, John, you've been complaining for at least twenty years," Officer Dunlap said, "afraid everyone is out to get you. Maybe, if you were a little nicer to people you wouldn't feel that one of them was trying to kill you."

"Get out of here," Mr. Sanford said. "You ladies can stay . . . for now. I'm calling Jayne."

The two officers left without another word. Mr. Sanford was about to go inside and leave us shivering on his porch.

"It's freezing out here," I said. "I don't mind so much for myself, but Mrs. Merriwether is recovering from a hospital stay for pneumonia. May we come inside?"

Maude coughed appropriately. She was always pale, so it wasn't a stretch to believe she'd recently been sick.

"All right, but you stay where I put you, and don't touch a thing."

We entered the small, dark house, and I for one had no intention of touching anything. My preference would have been to remain standing in the hall, but Mr. Sanford insisted we sit together on a lumpy sofa and wait for his next command.

I wondered if you could get bedbugs from a sofa.

Kate, Maude, and I huddled together. At least the house was warm, too warm actually. We took off coats, scarves and mittens and found the room an uncomfortable sauna.

John—I felt we were now on a first name basis—left the

room to use his landline in the hallway. We could hear everything he said.

"Jayne, what have you done?" Silence. "Why didn't you tell me?" More silence. "So I said no when you asked before—that was my choice." After another minute, John hung up the phone.

"Get your coats on," he said. "We're going to lunch. In your car. And I'm not paying. Just so you don't get any ideas about that."

"We have no illusions in that regard," I said. "Before we go, could you tell me about these photographs on the mantle? I see a lovely woman, your wife perhaps, standing next to a young girl. Who are they?"

"That ain't none of your business! I told Jayne this would never work, people butting into my life."

"We're trying to save you from harm," I said, "so we do need to butt into your life as you so eloquently put it."

John ignored me. He called his dog into the house, made sure she had food and water, and hurried us out the door.

We drove in silence and arrived at Dana's Kitchen at noon, right on time for our scheduled luncheon. The restaurant sat by itself surrounded by farmland. It had a veranda and outside seating that would be tempting on a summer day. We hurried inside to warm up and found Jayne waiting for us at the door. I wondered how forthright she'd be in front of John.

"Ah, Flo, what a pleasure," Jayne gushed.

I always have a little trouble with people who seem too happy to see me. She already knew Kate, and they hugged. She hadn't met Maude, so I introduced them.

Then Jayne did something I couldn't imagine. She hugged John. I wondered when John had last washed his overalls—or his hands, for that matter. Perhaps that's what came from working with animals. You didn't care how clean people were.

Even more amazing was the fact that John hugged her back.

Who was this man? I tried to see him in a different light. Clearly, he was difficult, but was he also a man capable of warm emotions? Perhaps Jayne simply loved all creatures great and small, like that book Kate was always hounding me to read. And perhaps John responded like a frightened animal to a gentle touch.

John chose a corner table and sat with his back to the wall. Apparently, he didn't want anyone sneaking up on him from behind and slitting his throat. I refrained from pointing out that someone could fire a shot through the outer wall of the restaurant or through a window and "finish him off" as he was so fond of saying.

We ordered lunch. John seemed to think this might be his last meal—he ordered two sandwiches, potato chips, and half a dozen cookies. "I like to take something back to Edna," he said.

When Maude looked puzzled, Jayne cleared up her confusion. "He named his dog after his wife who died many years ago. John likes to think his dog is his wife reincarnated, don't you, John?"

"You want to make me sound like I'm nuts, but I don't care. Edna has the same sweet temperament my wife had."

"I think it's actually possible," Kate said. "I'm not a full believer in reincarnation, but I'm not a disbeliever. And it is a very comforting thought."

Great. Now we had not one crazy person to contend with but possibly two. "You never mentioned you were studying Eastern religions," I said to her.

"You never asked," Kate said.

"In any case, I'm glad you've all met," Jayne said. "It saves us so much time. As you undoubtedly realize, John has his own unique take on the world."

I glanced over at John to see if he was reacting to her comments, but he seemed focused on the kitchen and when his food might appear.

Jayne smiled at me. "John doesn't care what I say. He assumes everyone is talking about him anyway. I didn't know him before his wife died, but people say he was a different man then, trusting, considerate, even generous. Not the man you see now—the one who's afraid of the world and irritated with everyone in it."

I guess that answered my question about how frank Jayne would be.

John didn't blink an eye. Unfortunately, Kate did.

"You may have met your match, Flo." Kate glanced at Jayne. "Flo could easily win the award for Boston's curmudgeon of the year. It's her Brahmin status that keeps her from receiving that title. People know she's too wealthy and well-connected to cross."

"Please," was all I said.

Maude rushed to my defense, such as it was. "Flo can be difficult. And she likes things the way she wants them. And she never finds them precisely to her liking. But—"

"I'm relieved there is a 'but,'" I said. "I was afraid we were going to waste a perfectly good lunch labeling me and John with terms we neither like nor deserve."

John shrugged his shoulders. "Best thing that ever happened to me, being called a curmudgeon. Don't have to see people and don't have to make small talk. People come into my shop, drop off their shoes, and pick them up when they're ready. No complaints in twenty years."

We all smiled at that, even John.

"What I was going to say," Maude spoke quietly, "was that Flo has been a great friend to me. Beyond saving my life, she's taught me to be courageous and enjoy all that life has to offer."

If I were a person who blushed, it's likely I would have

been beet red at that point. Instead, I squeezed her hand under the table where no one could see. I'd never admit it publicly, but Maude had changed me as well. If I wasn't careful, I'd become a sentimental old fool.

The food arrived, and everyone started eating, except Jayne. "I know what you mean about Flo." she said. "I couldn't agree more. John's the same way. I keep a dog shelter, and after I nursed his dog back to health, he made sure my shelter had everything it needed to survive. He encouraged me to go to vet school and said he'd pay for it."

"I'm sure that's all wonderful, but may we get on with things?" I asked.

I suspected John was as uncomfortable with this love fest as I was. He stuffed potato chips into his mouth and nodded at Jayne.

"By all means," Jayne said. "Do you want to tell them what's been happening, John, or do you want me to do it?"

"You," John mumbled, his mouth full of sandwich and chips.

"Very well. Stop me if I get something wrong—not that I really have to ask you to do that." Jayne put her fork down, took a sip of coffee and started.

"John has always been hyperaware of his environment—paranoid I'd have to say —so when things started to go wrong, no one really took him seriously. I know I didn't. I do remember the initial event happened on the first of December. It was the twentieth anniversary of his wife's death. I suppose that's why I remember the date. John always laid flowers on his wife's grave first thing in the morning on the anniversary of her death. Often he invited me along, but I couldn't make it that day."

"It's the same route I take every morning," John interrupted. "Narrow dirt road. No one around to bother me."

"That's right," Jayne said. "Same route. Same time of the

morning. John's habits are as fixed as his attitudes. So, I'd guess it was 5:30 in the morning?"

John nodded. "I'll tell it," he said. "It was still dark. Edna stopped abruptly, but I didn't. I stumbled into a pothole two feet wide by two feet deep. I could have broken an ankle, a knee, a hip."

"As it turned out, all he did was bruise himself," Jayne said.

"But that's not the point!" John said. "There hadn't been a pothole the morning before. Someone dug it fresh, just for me. They must have scattered the dirt from the hole or taken it with them."

Jayne nodded. "It did seem to be new. The police couldn't say if it was manmade or natural erosion, maybe a mini sinkhole. They got the Massachusetts Department of Transportation to check it out. They confirmed it was a pothole. No need to worry."

"Yeah, right. No need to worry," John said. "So what if some kook was out to finish me off—no big deal."

Jayne sighed and took a bite of her salad.

"Go on," I said.

"Really, Flo," Kate said, "let the woman eat. This is a marathon of information gathering, not a sprint."

Jayne smiled at Kate. "Thank you."

"Oh, please," I said. "This random politeness will be the death of me. Do what you need to do, Jayne, and then get on with the story."

John had finished his first sandwich and seemed to be waiting to start on his second. He nodded at Jayne. "I got it. The next attempt to do me in came four days later—on the anniversary of Edna's funeral. I was out in the woods, gathering kindling. It was a cold spell, and I was waiting to turn on my furnace—those utility companies want to rob you blind. They love boosting their rates in the wintertime. I got a good fireplace—I can stick close to it and stay pretty warm."

Jayne gave him a look I couldn't decipher, but she didn't speak.

"I'd left Edna at home. She'd be running after a squirrel, and I'd have my arms loaded with firewood. The last thing I wanted was a long cold hunt for my dog. I was heading back from the woods, going through the cemetery when a shot whizzed past my ear, I mean right past my ear. I hit the ground and crawled behind a gravestone. I stayed put on that frozen ground for twenty minutes. I think my would-be murderer thought maybe he could freeze me to death since he wasn't that good a shot."

John stopped. "You can tell the rest, Jayne." John picked up his second sandwich and bit into it as if he were starving.

"John called me when he finally got home. I insisted he call the police—there's no hunting allowed in those hills. The police came, searched the area and found a rifle shell casing once John pointed them in the right direction. So, he wasn't making that up. The police did check his rifle to make sure the bullet didn't come from his gun."

"And it didn't?" I had to ask. John seemed to be just squirrelly enough to do something like that to get the attention of the police.

"'Course not," John said. "You don't believe me, you can go home."

"I believe in the truth," I said.

"You weren't the only one to wonder about that," Jayne said, "but the bullet didn't come from John's rifle. He demanded the police put him under protective surveillance."

"And do you think they did that?" John said between mouthfuls. "Course not."

"What were they supposed to do, John?" Jayne asked. "Come to your house at 5:30 am and walk the dog with you? Spend the day with you?"

"Dudley Do-Right could do his damn job. Find out who wants me dead and stop them."

"That's one reason I read the article to you about Flo and her protection agency. It was almost a year old, but I knew you wouldn't notice that. I wanted to plant the idea that someone could help protect you."

"Yeah, and when you asked me, I said no over and over. You called her anyway."

"I didn't call until two more incidents happened. Ones that couldn't be called accidents. First the bad meat and then the bear trap. That one could have cost you your leg. That's when I called."

I asked for details of the last two events. They occurred on Mondays. John didn't work on Mondays. The bad meat seemed to be intended for John's dog. It was left just outside his door with a note that said, 'For Edna.' John snatched it up before Edna could get to it. He took a tiny bite to check it out and ended up in the emergency room with his stomach pumped.

I couldn't remain silent. "You took a bite of meat you found outside your door? Why in the world would you do that?"

"It looked as if someone had left a perfectly good steak for my dog to enjoy. I thought maybe it was Jayne, an early Christmas present for Edna. It was cooked, still warm, so I knew someone had just dropped it off. I took a tiny bite to make sure it was safe, and then I called Jayne. She said she hadn't left it and I should keep it away from my dog until she had a chance to check it out."

"The meat was full of arsenic," Jayne said. "The police claimed it was probably some neighbor angry at John for letting his dog run wild. But Edna is a sweetheart. That's when I knew someone was trying to torment John, maybe kill him. The bear trap confirmed it."

"It went off seconds before I reached it," John said. "It was near the big house at the top of the hill. Sometimes I go there just to keep an eye on things. Someone or something snapped it. I didn't find any animal in it when I got there, but it could have been my foot in that trap."

"John, do you have any idea who might be doing this to you?" I asked.

He shook his head vehemently. "I don't bother people. I stay away from them. I go to my shop four days a week, and then stay home Saturday, Sunday, Monday to recover from all the stupid folks I have to deal with. 'Why are my shoes falling apart? Why is my heel worn so crooked? Why can't you replace the leather on the top of the shoe?' I'm not a shoe maker, I'm a shoe repairer. I can take only so many questions."

Since he was going down this unlikely road, I decided to go with him. "Was a customer ever livid with you?"

"They all were. Didn't like my price or didn't like the time it took to make a repair. But they never complained about my work, and they never stopped coming with their shoes."

"So," I said, "it's highly unlikely a customer would be interested in 'finishing you off.'"

John sat quietly for a minute. He was done eating most of his second sandwich and asked for a doggy bag for the rest. Finally, he spoke.

"You're not as dumb as you look," he said to me. "No customer would want to kill me. I run the best shoe repair shop on the Cape. People come to me from Chatham. No, it's not a customer."

"Excellent," I said. "So we can leave your clientele off our suspect list. Who might want to kill or harm you?"

"A neighbor," John said. "Everyone on my street wants me to clean up my act, gentrify my house. Why? I'm not selling. It's just the way I like it. They say their children are afraid to walk by my place. So, don't walk by it."

"Anyone else?" I asked.

"John makes a lot of complaints to Town Hall," Jayne said. "He's ticked off nearly every government official complaining about his taxes or parking or the state of the roads around here. They brought his name up for discussion in a Falmouth town meeting. People agreed he was wasting everyone's time with his constant complaints, but the selectmen said there was nothing to be done. After all, John isn't the only curmudgeon in Falmouth."

"I was thinking about something more personal," I said. "A grudge a friend or a relative might have against him."

"Yes, that makes more sense," Jayne said. "What about that, John?"

"Don't have any relatives or friends," John said.

"What about that girl I saw in your photographs?" I asked.

"I knew I never should have invited you inside. I'm too soft-hearted. Should have left you old girls outside to freeze."

"What about the girl in the photograph?" Jayne asked. "I don't even know her name. I know she was someone your wife was very fond of—you can tell that from the pictures."

John remained silent.

Jayne waved at the waiter for the bill, and then turned to us. "John told me the young woman was a relative of his wife's but never said more about her."

"Goddaughter, I told you. I never said relative." John sounded angry.

"Goddaughter then," Jayne said.

"Will you tell us about her now?" I asked.

"She was a hateful girl. I certainly didn't know that at first. Didn't know it at all until my wife died."

"And yet you kept the photographs on your wall," I said. "I know if I had someone who betrayed me, the first thing I'd do is destroy their pictures."

"I didn't say she betrayed me. Don't put words in my

mouth. I kept the photos because those are the only pictures I have of Edna. The girl was a liar, that's what she was. My wife couldn't see through her, but I could."

We waited, but John seemed to be done.

"John, we can't help you if you don't tell us everything," Maude said. "Who is this girl?"

"Name's Jennifer. Jennifer Emerson. Bad blood in that family. My wife thought Jennifer was different, but she wasn't. She was responsible for my wife's death. I'm not saying more. You can't protect me? Fine, I don't give a damn."

I'm sure we all looked shocked, but John was done talking. He sat silent, his head down.

Maude put a hand on his arm, and he didn't shake it off.

"I have no idea what happened," she said, "but I'd like to tell you a story of my own. My granddaughter married a man I thought was good and kind. Like your wife, I couldn't see through him. The man wanted to kill me, but he didn't succeed, thanks to Flo. You need to tell us all about this girl, so we can help you."

"I can't right now. I have to think this through."

"All right," I said. "Think it over. But don't forget that Monday, the day your would-be assassin likes to do you harm, is two days away."

John looked up and nodded.

Jayne took the bill from the waiter and refused to allow me to pay. "I hired you, remember?"

"Very well. An unnecessary show of pride," I said.

"To you, maybe," Jayne said, "but not to me. I've worked for every penny I have. It's one reason I don't think I can take John's generous offer for vet school. And why I can't take yours. For you, perhaps, money doesn't mean much, but for me it means a great deal."

Kate looked me in the eye. "Well said."

"John, I have to ask you something before we leave." This

was from Jayne who was putting on her coat. John looked up at her as if he were only slowly coming back to the present. "It isn't about the girl— I'll leave that to Flo. It's about gathering wood for your fireplace. That's what you said you were doing when you were almost shot, didn't you?"

"So?" John asked.

"You haven't used your fireplace in years. You said the chimney was cracked and it wasn't safe. You couldn't have been gathering wood for your fireplace that morning. What were you doing?"

John hesitated for a couple of seconds, then he spoke.

"When you went to the big house, you saw the fireplace, noticed the wood. I'd stacked it there. Did it every morning this winter. People were staying in that house. I paid for their electricity and I brought them wood, a little food."

"You must have known who they were," I said.

"No, I didn't. But I'm a Christian man. I saw my duty and I did it."

Kate let out an exasperated sigh. "How did you know the people in the house weren't using it as a place to do drugs, or didn't you care about that either? You could have put your neighbors at great risk. A person on drugs will steal anything from anyone. I don't suppose you mentioned this to the police."

"No. I knew these people weren't addicts. I never found a needle, other drug paraphernalia. They kept the kitchen area neat and left the rest of the house alone."

"John," I said. "You are testing our credulity. You, a man who wants everyone to mind his own business, go out of your way to help some squatters stay warm and fed."

"It's got nothing to do with my future murder, and I'm done talking."

We stood, put our coats on, and headed for the door. Jayne took me aside.

"I'll try to see what I can find out from John and call you later. The Emersons are well known around here for causing trouble—at least back in the day. Lived off Old Dock Road—that's all I know."

We parted, and Kate drove us back to our house where we regrouped in the living room.

"We have to find out about this Jennifer person," I said, "and about her family. We also need to see who owns the house that John seems to be taking such special care of. He wouldn't do that for some random person—he hates strangers."

"I'll check with Town Hall," Kate said. "They'll have records of house ownership. The Jennifer issue sounds more like your department. Yours and Maude's. I'll try to get an address for the place near Old Dock Road and see if neighbors know anything about the family. But what we need are some old timers and gossip. "

"We saw some old men sitting outside the West Falmouth Market when we took a tour of the town. Near the library wasn't it? Maybe they'd like to talk to us—or at least to you, Maude. You're better at getting people to open up than I am."

We bundled up and set out on our assignments.

A group of men sat huddled outside the market despite the chill in the air.

"Leave us at the library," I said, "and we'll walk back here. I don't want them to think we are wealthy outsiders and clam up on us."

Kate dropped us and drove off in the opposite direction. Maude and I headed for the market. We stepped inside a quaint and lovely store with rows of gourmet items for the inhabitants of West Falmouth. Along one wall stretched a long counter filled with home-baked pastries and coffee urns. I'm not one to pass on good food.

I loaded a plate with a cheese danish and a blueberry muffin. Maude bought a brownie. We headed outdoors with our coffee and plates. Fortunately, the three small tables were filled—two of them pulled together to accommodate a group of six older men.

Perfect.

Maude and I stood looking a little helpless and definitely cold. I watched as Maude smiled at one man and wobbled ever so slightly.

"Here, here," the man said. "Let me help you. Make room, guys." He took her plate and helped her sit beside him. I squeezed in on the other side of him, as the rest of the men made room.

We commented on the quality of the food and the coffee, and then about the charm of West Falmouth. The men seemed happy to talk about the history of the town. Turns out it was an old Quaker enclave. It also turned out, the Emersons were well-known trouble makers.

"Used to be leaders around here," one man named Robert said. "Respected. Then things went south for the family. Too much hard drinking, not enough livelihood."

"Gambling," another said.

"Hmm," I said. Often that was all you needed to say to keep people talking.

"Grandfather's in jail I think for murder or assault. He was a bad one."

"Edmund Emerson," a man said, sitting near the end of the table."I knew him from way back. Always in and out of trouble. I'd be surprised if he was still alive."

"You know if he had a daughter?" I asked. "Named Jennifer?"

All eyes stared at me.

"How would you know about her?" Robert asked. "You said you're not from around here."

"We're not, but Jayne Winston is a friend," I said, "and she has a friend John Sanford who knew Jennifer."

"Jennifer was a sweet girl growing up," Robert said. "She took to drink later on like her father and died a couple of months ago. I think she had a child. Might still be around. Any of you know about a child?"

The other men shook their heads.

We finished our coffee and our conversation.

Jennifer was dead. I wondered if John knew.

Next stop was the library. It was an old one with paneled wood walls and friendly librarians. We sought out the one that appeared to be the oldest and sang the praises of the library.

"So welcoming," Maude said.

And it was true. It would be the perfect place to curl up with a good book, but that wasn't why we were there. Honesty seemed to be the best policy. We explained what we were doing in West Falmouth a few days before Christmas.

Agnes, the librarian, stood with her mouth open until we were done.

"We all know John," she said, and the other woman at her side nodded. "Everyone around here does. He complains when the weather's too cold."

"Or too hot," Agnes said. "But the idea that anyone would want to murder John—that's absurd. He's really a harmless man, and we're all scared to death he may decide to retire some day—then where will we get our shoes repaired? I've known John for thirty years, went to his wedding."

Maude and I looked at each other. We'd lucked onto a gold mine.

"You knew his wife, Edna?"

"I went to high school with her and John. I remember Edna was flattered by the attention he gave her. He was a sweetheart in those days, a romantic I'd have to say. They were very much in love. They wanted a big family, but the children never came. Then this girl entered their lives."

"Jennifer Emerson?" I asked.

"Yes, that's the one. Edna was a rescuer, and this girl needed rescuing—that much was clear. Her father couldn't hold his liquor or his temper. Edna wanted to get Jennifer away from him, but before she could do that, she died."

"Do you know what happened?

Agnes shook her head. "It was all so sudden. John never spoke of it except to say it was Jennifer's fault that his wife died. He became bitter, never got over his loss."

When I asked about the house on the hill, Agnes just shook her head. "Edna told me she and John were saving up to buy a house, but she never told me where it was."

We'd learned a few things, but we still had our mystery about the house and about what had happened to Edna.

KATE PICKED us up at the library an hour later. "I've got information. The old house off Old Dock Road is still there. Neighbors say the old man comes back to it when he's out of jail or out of liquor. Rants and raves calling for his granddaughter, Amber, and then disappears again."

"Amber," I said, "so that's the granddaughter."

"Apparently," Kate said. "And you want to know who owns the house on the top of the hill?"

"John?" I asked.

"You're not far off the mark," Kate said. "Apparently, John bought the house twenty years ago, put it in his wife's name. She left the house to Jennifer when she died."

"And now?" I asked. "Now, who owns it?"

"No idea. Jennifer's will hasn't been probated," Kate said, "if there even was a will."

"Maybe," Maude said, "when we tell John what we know, he'll open up to us about the rest—if Jayne is there with us."

Jayne agreed to meet us at his house.

We drove to John's house and waited outside until Jayne arrived. John didn't act surprised to see us. "I'm ready to talk," he said. "I heard from some men around the village you've been asking about me. I guess you really do want to help."

He directed us into the living room to the sofa while he sat in a sagging armchair with his head in his hands.

John rubbed his craggy face and leaned forward. "That house is special to me. Edna and I were going to buy the house and fix up. I'd saved up money, and she had too. She worked as a visiting nurse and went around the community, wherever she was needed. That's how she met Jennifer.

"We'd saved enough money to buy the house outright, and I bought it as a surprise for her, put it in her name. Then she up and died before we could move in."

"Of what?" I asked. "She must have been a young woman."

"She was forty. Died just before her forty-first birthday— she was born on Christmas."

"A Christmas angel," Maude said softly.

John looked at Maude with the slightest smile on his face. "That's what I always called her, my Christmas angel. I was nothing before I met her, and I'm nothing without her."

"How long were you married?" I asked.

"Ten years. The only good ten years of my life."

"How did she die, John?' I asked.

"My fault . . . and Jennifer's. Lying Jennifer's."

John put his face in his hands. "Edna wasn't feeling well. Flu-like. Headache. I told her to stay home from work. She said she would. I asked Jennifer to check on Edna while I was at the shop. Jennifer said she'd be happy to stop in. She'd call me if anything was wrong. That's how we left it."

The labyrinth of lines on John's forehead deepened. His body tightened, and his face grew more jagged and taut. It was like watching a time bomb tick down the last few seconds.

"Jennifer never stopped by. I called the house around noon and no one answered. I came home, and Edna wasn't making sense. I took her to the hospital and she died hours later. Triple E."

"Eastern Equine Encephalitis," Jayne said. "A terrible disease, rare, comes from mosquitoes and shows up in the summer and early fall. Not in December."

"That's why it was my fault," John said. "Edna and I would take a long walk every evening down by the bogs when the weather was warm. The weather was mild that year into late November. There were days when Edna said she was too tired from work, and I insisted a walk would do her good. I'm responsible for her getting sick, and Jennifer is responsible for her death."

"John, once she got sick there was nothing to be done," Jayne said. "There's no treatment, no cure. And if she had survived it's likely she would have had brain damage. She wouldn't be the woman you'd known before."

"Maybe. But I would have taken care of her. She would have been at my side. And if Jennifer had done what she promised, my Edna wouldn't have suffered alone."

"Why didn't Jennifer come?" I asked.

"At first she said she had, and Edna was fine. I knew that wasn't true. Edna felt bad when I left her—she didn't miraculously recover. Later, Jennifer admitted her boyfriend offered to take her Christmas shopping in Boston, so she went."

"How old was she at the time?" Maude asked.

"Sixteen. It was a Saturday, and she could have come," John said.

"Sixteen," Kate said. "I remember what I was like at sixteen. What were you like at that age, John?"

He flinched. "I was a rabble rouser in my day. But that isn't the point. She said she'd come and she didn't."

"And it wouldn't have made one bit of difference if she had

come," I said. "From what Jayne says, your wife would still be dead. It was no one's fault. Not yours and not Jennifer's."

"I'll bet Jennifer felt horrible," Maude said.

"She claimed she did, once she finally told me the truth. We haven't spoken since."

"Do you know what happened to her?" I asked.

"Don't know. Don't care."

"She died," I said. "A couple of months ago."

John looked genuinely shocked. "Dead?"

The news seemed to take all the stuffing out of him. "I heard that she'd died, but I didn't believe it. I didn't want to believe it." He rubbed his hand over his face. "Edna loved that girl as if she were the child we were never able to have. That's why I can't take down the pictures. Edna would have brought her to live with us, but Jennifer's father wouldn't allow it. I'm glad Edna didn't live to hear this—it would have crushed her.

"In the past month I thought I must be losing my mind. For real. I thought I saw Jennifer near the big house one day. Just the way she looked twenty years ago. She looked right through me. I couldn't tell if she was angry or scared. That's when I first believed she might be dead. It might be her ghost I saw."

"You knew Jennifer owned the house?" Kate asked.

"'Course I knew. Edna and I had no secrets. She asked me first—would I mind if anything happened to her, could she leave the house to Jennifer? I told her it was her house, and I'd never want to live it in without her."

"You must have figured out someone was living in the house," Maude said.

"I did. I decided that I needed to forgive Jennifer. Maybe that's why she appeared before me as a ghost. To make me a better man. I thought maybe her soul would rest easier if I took care of the house and whoever was living in it."

"Did you know Jennifer had a daughter?" Kate asked. "A daughter named Amber."

"No," John said. "You think she's the one I saw? Not a spirit?"

"Could be," I said. "Do you think she might be the one wishing to harm you?"

"Why? Jennifer never tried to harm me. Why would her daughter do that? She ain't the one," John said. "Jennifer's dead—Edna will never forgive me."

Suddenly, he broke down. Big, gulping sobs.

"All Jennifer ever wanted to do was to apologize to me, beg me to forgive her. And I wouldn't do it. Now, it's too late."

Jayne stood and put a hand on his shoulder.

John had lost his hard edges. He was not so much a broken man as a grieving one.

Jayne said she'd stay with John for a while, so we left.

"What will we do now?" Maude asked.

"I think we need to find out who's living in the house," I said.

Kate drove us up and parked behind a cluster of pitch pine that would hide us from the house and the road. We walked quietly to the front door.

"Yoo-hoo," I called out. "Anyone home?" And then I called, "Amber? Are you there?"

For a moment, nothing, then the slow padding of stockinged feet from the back of the house.

"Who are you?" a young woman asked. She looked to be in her late teens. She was small, and I wondered if she was the creature who'd disappeared down the stairs the last time we were there.

"I'm Florence Wellington, and these are my associates Maude Merriwether and Kate Fitzhugh. Who are you, my dear?"

"I'm no one's dear," she said curtly. "I happen to be Jennifer Emerson's daughter—Amber. She owned this house and left it to me when she died."

"You're living here now?" I asked.

"I won't answer another question until you tell me why you're here. You were here before, weren't you?"

Maude stood on the porch shivering. It seemed to do the trick.

Amber's stern features softened. "You're too old to be standing on the porch in this weather. Come in."

We followed her through the empty hallway to the kitchen where she had a heater on full blast.

"Those can be dangerous, you know," I said. "Why not use the fireplace? You have plenty of wood, I see."

"The last time you were in the house you made a fire. Then the police arrived. I won't let that happen again."

"Why not, if you own the house?" I asked.

"Because with my luck, John Sanford will show up. He's crazy."

"You know John?" Maude asked. "He's odd but he's also frightened. Afraid someone is after him."

Amber nodded and remained silent.

"John is the reason we're here. Someone's been threatening him this past month. He's had several serious accidents, and he's afraid someone is trying to kill him. Do you know anything about that?"

Amber looked like a very young child caught with her hand in the cookie jar. She flushed and wouldn't answer.

Maude put a hand on her arm. "What is it, Amber?"

"He's paranoid about everything," she said. "He thought my mother killed his wife. Why would you believe anything he says?"

"Because we think he's telling the truth this time," I said.

"I don't have to tell you anything. You're the one trespassing on my property. Get out or I'll call the police."

"Be my guest," I said, handing her my phone.

She didn't take it. "I don't like the police any more than I like you."

"It seems you and John have something in common," I said.

"Just get out of here and leave me alone."

I certainly wasn't about to leave. "We have been employed to save John Sanford's life. I have the feeling you know exactly what I'm talking about. Are you responsible for what's been happening to him?"

Maude gave me that look of hers that meant I was coming on too strong. "Amber,

she said, "I don't believe you are responsible for what's happening, but perhaps you know something that might help us save his life."

Amber stared at Maude, her brown eyes filling with tears. Before she could say anything, we heard someone stumbling up the back steps.

"Oh God, please leave now!" she yelled at us.

Kate pulled me into the hallway, and Maude followed. We closed the swinging door that led to the kitchen and listened.

We could hear Amber opening the back door.

Someone bellowed from outside. "Help me. Help me, you idiot. My foot is stuck in the damn step. You said you'd get that fixed."

"I told you to stay away from here until I had," Amber shouted back.

"Get me inside. I'm freezing."

"I can't manage you, Grandpa. You're drunk again. You promised."

Kate, Maude and I rushed through the kitchen door. We ran to the back porch and helped Amber pull her grandfather inside.

He was decidedly drunk. He lurched to the mattress on the floor and collapsed there. He started to say something to

Maude and me, but his speech was too slurred to understand. Eventually, he gave up, rolled over, and started snoring.

"He's destroyed every good thing in my life," Amber said, and she began to cry. Maude sat her on a kitchen chair and put an arm around her. On the kitchen table lay a nearly complete quilted lap rug. So this was what the scraps of material were for.

Amber saw me staring at her handiwork. "Someone has been trying to help me—bringing me food and wood. I wanted to give them a Christmas present. It's the least I can do. They always manage to come when I'm at school, so I have no idea who it might be."

"This is lovely work, my dear," Maude said.

"I used an old shirt of Grandfather's. He'll never miss it."

I turned off the space heater and started a fire. Someone had carefully built it, and all it needed was a match to the kindling. Then I brought her a glass of water. "Why are you here, Amber?"

"I'm not camped out here to kill John Sanford, if that's what you imagine. I'm here to stop my grandfather from doing it. My mother, Jennifer, had one wish and that was to talk to John and beg his forgiveness. I assume you know the story of how John's wife died. He never stopped blaming my mother for her death. Never.

"Mr. Sanford is a mean old man, but he's met his match in my grandfather. They knew each other in school and hated one another from the start. Too much alike I think, only Grandfather took to drink and Mr. Sanford never touched a drop.

"My mother took after my granddad, drinking too much, and always said I was the only good thing that had ever happened to her. My mother died two months ago of cirrhosis. That's when my grandfather turned his rage on Mr. Sanford. He blamed him for my mom's miserable life. He swore he'd make Mr. Sanford suffer and then die for all the harm he'd done to our family."

"So you tried to stop him," I said.

"Yes. My mother didn't hate John Sanford. She loved him. He and his wife had taken her in, gotten her away from my grandfather when he got drunk and belligerent. When his wife died and Mr. Sanford wouldn't see or speak to my mother, she gave up trying to make a good life."

"But Edna left your mother this house," I said.

"My mother couldn't bear to live here—so close to someone who hated her."

"You mean John?" Maude asked.

"Yes. It's odd. I saw him in the woods a month ago. He looked shocked. I didn't speak and he didn't either."

"You look like your mother," Kate said. "Exactly like her from the photos we saw in John's house."

"I've never seen those photos, but I wondered if he recognized me. He stared at me, then called his dog and headed down the hill."

"You decided to live in the house—why?" I asked.

"It was the future my mother never got to have. I want to make it beautiful again, bit by bit, make it a sober house, perhaps. My mother would have liked that."

"How old are you?" I asked.

"Seventeen. I'm out of school for Christmas, not playing truant if that's what you're wondering. I'm a straight A student —I'm going to make something of myself."

"I can believe that," Maude said.

"Someday, I'll have the money to do what I want. But first I have to deal with my grandfather. He's doing what he's always done—trying to destroy anything that's good."

"You think he means to kill John?" Kate asked.

"Yes. And it's up to me to stop it."

"Why didn't you call the police? Maude asked.

"He's my flesh and blood. I can't do that."

"How did you discover what he meant to do to John?" I asked.

"That wasn't hard. When Grandfather is drunk, which is most of the time, he rants. When my mother died, all he could talk about was making John Sanford suffer. Grandfather is a strong man, and when he's sober, he's dangerous. I followed him.

"I could see that Mr. Sanford might be in danger. I saw Grandfather dig a pothole, mumbling about how John would break a leg when he fell into it. I planned to fill it back up the next morning, but I didn't realize how early Mr. Sanford took his daily walks. Then the gun. I saw grandfather grab his rifle when he saw John walking in the cemetery. I followed him and knocked him over when he took aim at John. That made Grandfather furious. He turned the rifle on me, and I thought he might just kill me."

"Oh, Lord," Maude said. She hugged Amber tight. "You poor girl."

"Then he did something I didn't know even he could do. He doctored some meat and left it out for John's dog. I was about to grab it, but John opened the door before I could get to it. He saw the meat and the note. Then he picked it up, smelled it, and tasted it. Later I heard it made him plenty sick."

"And the bear trap?" I asked.

"I saw Grandfather set it. I snapped it just before Mr. Sanford could walk into it. He didn't see me, but he heard it and knew it was meant for him."

"We think he has plans for this Monday—the day John stays home from work. Do you know what they are?" I asked.

"I have an idea. I think my Grandfather plans to kill the one creature John loves best, his dog, and then he plans to kill John by setting his house on fire. He's got kerosene stored on the back porch. I thought I could find some way to stop him if he really meant to do it."

Mr. Emerson continued to snore on the mattress.

"I'll take care of that," Kate said.

Kate scrubbed out the containers and replaced the kerosene with water in the same cans while Amber's grandfather slept on. The kerosene smell remained strong, but Kate assured us the canisters would not start a fire.

The three of us brought Amber to our car to have a much-needed talk. Her grandfather was a danger. The safest place for him was in jail. He'd get sobered up there and wouldn't be a threat to anyone. Better a grandfather in jail than a grandfather who was a murderer. We had to call in the police.

Reluctantly, Amber agreed.

We left her at the big house and drove down the road to John's. We told him what was going to happen on Monday. The police agreed to go along with our plan. John said he'd leave the dog with Jayne at her shelter and play along.

It was late Monday night when Mr. Emerson showed up. Kate, Maude, and I stationed ourselves in the woods behind John's house, near the police. Emerson looked around for the dog, calling out for her with a poisoned treat. When she didn't appear, he gave up and began to pour the canisters of water around the base of the wooden house. He checked to make sure John was asleep in his bed by peering in the bedroom window. Then he lit his match and backed away, virtually into the arms of Officer Dunlap.

Emerson looked stunned. First by the fire that didn't erupt and then by the handcuffs Officer Dunlap clapped onto his wrists. "I didn't do anything," he sputtered as two more officers joined Dunlap and grabbed the cans he'd dropped.

Maude, Kate, and I appeared once the police had him under control. "We all saw it," I said.

John came out of the house, a coat over his pajamas. He

stared at Emerson. "I don't care so much about me—I know you're mad at me, but you were gonna kill my dog. She never did a thing to you."

Emerson ignored him.

"It's that granddaughter of mine, isn't it? She told you," he said, railing at the officers. "Couldn't keep her mouth shut. Never could keep her mouth shut."

Emerson was stone cold sober, and he was furious. It took all three officers to muscle him into the squad car.

Amber couldn't bear to be there, so we called her once it was all over. We told her as much of it as she wanted to hear—that nothing bad had happened and that her grandfather had been taken to jail. We left out what he said about her.

Later, from us, John learned the whole story of Jennifer's miserable life, and I've never seen a more unhappy man. His guilt seemed to overwhelm him. He closed his shop, and for two months he stayed in his home, shades drawn.

Jayne visited him daily and nursed him back to health, the same way she'd nursed his dog. She brought him soup and watched as he ate it. Amber helped in her own way from afar. She was stunned to hear that the man who had helped in the house was John and that the Christmas gift she had made was for him.

John cried when he received her gift and read her note.

"I hope this will keep you warm," Amber wrote. "My mother would be happy to know that I have finally met you."

He didn't speak of the past at first, but he used Amber's lap rug every day. Eventually, he asked Jayne questions about the girl and seemed eager to hear how she was doing.

When he was well, he helped Amber fix up the big house. He had enough money and the skills to do most of the work himself.

Eventually, he became a caretaker of the place and lived in a small bedroom with his dog. Amber insisted on that. When

Amber graduated from high school the following spring, John gave her the money to go to college—a small school called Clark University in Worcester, Massachusetts, a school that "changed people's lives."

It did that for Amber. It let her be far enough away to lead her own life and close enough to visit John once a month. Amber's grandfather died in jail, a sober man. Amber said they reconciled before he died, but we never knew the details of that meeting. We didn't need to, as Maude pointed out. That was their personal story not ours.

We all grew to be good friends. Kate drove us down to the Cape when we were not off saving lives. John and I sparred when it was appropriate and sometimes when it wasn't. In the summer, we spent a month on the Cape close to Amber and John. Amber made good on creating a safe house for women in need of it.

And we advertised in the Falmouth Enterprise each summer and distributed our cards to all the businesses in town —just in case someone needed protection while we were there.

THE END

3

CALIFORNIA DREAMIN'

"You are going to love this trip," Kate said. "I grew up in California and almost went to UC San Diego until a guy persuaded me to go to Oberlin instead. I thought I was headed to the East—somehow I didn't register that Ohio was located in the Midwest."

"First off, I'm not going to love it," I told Kate. "I like my Christmases crisp and cool."

Kate couldn't seem to resist. "To match your personality," she said, winking at Maude.

Maude covered her mouth with her hand and let out the tiniest giggle.

I continued as if Kate hadn't interrupted me. "Secondly, your sense of geography is appalling! At least you landed in a good school and managed to dump that weird boyfriend before he caused you lasting harm."

"Not a boyfriend, Flo, a representative of Oberlin. It was good for me in the end. It's how I got involved in the biathlon.

That *was* because of a boyfriend who was obsessed with skiing and shooting. Anyway, you'll enjoy the scenery and the stops we have planned. And you know, as I suggested, we could fly."

"No, we could not. We have an excellent automobile with friends to see along the way. We were told to arrive one week from tomorrow on December 23rd, so we'll drive."

I was certainly not about to expose my fear of flying to these two. Or to anyone for that matter. Never reveal your weaknesses—that was my father's mantra. As a Boston Brahmin, the community required us to appear strong and invincible, like Queen Elizabeth, poor dear. We'd just finished the second season of *The Crown,* and I had a great deal more sympathy for the old girl.

"Now, may we get back to the matter at hand," I said. I looked at Kate, daring her to challenge my decision to drive. She knew better than to do that.

We all sat around my dining room table finishing a lovely pumpkin pie—the final remnants of Thanksgiving. By all, I mean Kate, Maude and me. We were the official members of ODPA—the Old Dames Protection Agency. Kate was much too young to be official, so she belonged by special dispensation on my part.

The truth was I never minded a little warmth on my old bones. We'd had an early snow in Boston and the thought of warmer weather on the West Coast was enticing—no matter what I told them. Of course, with my luck we'd probably run into a rampant fire or the kind of heat that left you sweaty and panting for breath. I didn't mind so much for myself—I was only 82. But Maude, at 83, was too old to get overheated.

"Do you mind if I turn down the thermostat, dear?" Maude asked. "The room is a little too warm for me."

"Turn it to zero for all I care. I want you comfortable in my own house. Don't worry about me."

Kate left the table and returned with a cashmere throw.

"Wrap this around you. You aren't coming down with something, are you, Flo?"

Kate was in her early forties and always healthy as a horse. She seemed to love flaunting that fact.

"No, I am not coming down with something! I never come down with anything. I just got chilled when Maude and I walked through the Public Garden this afternoon."

"It was lovely," Maude said. "I'm so glad we went out. The Christmas decorations are everywhere, and I do love Christmas."

Finally, something we could all agree on. "As do I. And it seems once again we are needed to prevent a murder during the holiday season."

My cook, Marianne, cleared the table and left the centerpiece of elves frolicking in a snowy forest setting. Normally, I would be aghast at such sentimentality, but my father had made it for me when I was five. It sat as our Christmas centerpiece this year. Marianne brought us more decaf coffee, and I pulled the letter from my handbag. Like the queen, I always had my handbag at my side. "I know we've read it a hundred times, but let's look it over once more. It's handwritten, so unusual these days."

I put it on the table where the three of us could study it.

"Old-fashioned," Kate said, "but highly legible."

"In cursive," Maude added. "We won't see that in a few years."

I looked at Maude, a little surprised. "So you know about the decision to eliminate cursive from the school curriculum?"

"Of course, I do," Maude said. "I read the papers just like you—only I read mine online."

"Don't get me started," I said. "The Internet. Humbug. They find out everything about you, so they can sell you more of what you never needed in the first place. Ridiculous."

"Are you done?" Kate asked.

"For now." I looked over the handwriting. "Very elegant. It looks like a woman's hand and yet it's signed by a man—E. Elgin Smith. What have you found out about him, Kate?"

"Not a great deal. It's a pen name for someone who's written thirteen rough-and-tumble mysteries. His protagonist is a cowboy detective who settled in California in the1930s. The author's real name has remained a secret, kind of like Elena Ferrante."

"Perhaps because the author is in fact female," I said. "A cowboy mystery might not sell as well, if readers knew it was written by a woman. I've always wondered if Ferrante was a man. The descriptions of female friendship are entirely foreign to me. No one who behaved as these 'friends' did to each other could ever be a friend of mine. More like an enemy in plain sight."

Kate stifled a yawn.

"Am I keeping you up, Kate?"

"Sorry. It's just that I've heard that criticism a hundred times before, and I actually like the books."

"That is not to your credit, my dear, or to the women's movement."

"Please, Flo, can we not go there?" Kate asked. "We still have so much ground to cover before we leave in the morning."

If I hadn't been sleepy myself, I might have enjoyed a good argument with Kate, but she had a point.

"Back to the letter. We agree this letter is most likely written by a woman, then." All heads nodded. "It has an old-fashioned quality to it. Not just the cursive writing, but the choice of words—'would you be so kind'—etc." Heads nodded once more. "If I'm not mistaken our writer is closer in age to Maude and me, than to you, Kate."

"Agreed," Kate said.

"He or she, E. Elgin Smith, has been writing for thirty years," Maude said, "so it's unlikely she's a spring chicken."

"You could find no address, no agent, Kate?" I asked.

"I did contact the agent, a Jeremy Lambert," Kate said. "The letter was mailed through his address. He sounded surprised to hear from me and said he could give out no personal data."

"Surprised how?"

Kate remained uncharacteristically silent.

"Actually," Maude said, "I contacted the agent. I finished Smith's last book—it was really quite good—so Kate and I agreed that I might be the best person to try to make contact. An excited fan and all that."

"Maude, you didn't tell him about what the letter said, did you?" I asked.

Maude looked as if she might be about to cry. "Not at first. But when he wouldn't give me any information, I just said I was a little worried about the author. Then he asked why. He could tell I was fumbling for a response. I said, the author hadn't published a book in many years, and I wondered why."

"I see. Did he buy that?" I asked.

"I doubt it. He seemed suspicious about my call and ended the conversation abruptly."

"Hmm. The good news is you didn't tell him about the threat. The bad news is he knows someone is worried about E. Elgin Smith. We shall hope he is not the murderer in waiting."

"I'm so sorry, Flo. I can't lie as easily as you do. It's my weakness—if someone asks, I usually have to tell them some form of the truth."

"It's not the end of the world, Maude," I said, "at least I hope it's not."

I saw tears in Maude's eyes and relented. "No more worries, Maude. What's done is done. It's most likely she confided in her agent about the attempts on her life, and that's why he hung up on you. Kate, will you read the letter, so I don't have to get out my glasses? I want to hear it out loud."

Kate picked up the letter.

"Dear Miss Wellington:

I am desperately in need of your help. Someone is intent on killing me,

and in doing it in a way that reflects the most inhumane and cruel process.

The person wants me to be aware of my impending death by choosing

a single element from each of my books. Each reflects the moment before

death, and then each attempt stops before I'm actually killed.

THE BOOKS ARE CHOSEN in random order, so I cannot prepare for the next assault. I assume the murderer means to go through all of them before actually killing me, but, of course, I can't be certain of that.

I HAVE WRITTEN THIRTEEN BOOKS, and I have almost died seven times so far. The police think

this is a publicity stunt because my last book sold poorly and I can't find a publisher for my most recent one. This is no publicity stunt. I am in fear for my life.

I KNOW you take on difficult cases, and I know you have saved people like me. If you will be so kind as to take my case, I will pay all your expenses. I will meet you at the Huntley Hotel in Santa Monica where I have booked rooms under the assumed name of E. Jones beginning December 23rd.

.   .   .

I should still be alive by then as the attacks happen every few days or so. I won't leave my home until the 22nd in hopes of confusing my would-be murderer.

Yours in life and death,

Elgin

"Did we learn anything new this time through?" Kate asked.

"She sent the letter by overnight express," I said, "meaning she wants us there sooner rather than later. And yet she gave us a specific time to arrive. She naively thinks she can keep the murderer at bay until we come and that somehow he won't trace her to the Huntley. I am curious about why she didn't hire a private detective in Los Angeles—I'm sure they have plenty of those and some of them are undoubtedly reputable."

"Perhaps, she's as intent about keeping her identity a secret as she is about keeping herself alive," Maude said. "Maybe she was afraid a local PI would leak something to the press."

"You may be right," I said. "On the other hand I don't understand why her murderer doesn't reveal the author's true name. Our Elgin Smith would undoubtedly find that quite cruel."

"Perhaps the murderer is waiting for the grand finale," Kate said. "Murder and then the great reveal."

"All possible," I said. "It's also possible this is nothing more than a publicity stunt, as the police suspect."

"You might be right," Maude said. "The last book sold

poorly as the author admits, and her publisher went out of business. When I asked why there were no new books coming out, Smith's agent acknowledged he's been unable to find anyone interested in continuing the series."

"The author may be looking for a way to bring herself back to life, so to speak," I said.

"Nothing better than a threatened demise to do that. Have the papers picked up the story?"

"Only the rags," Kate said. "The legitimate papers seem to think it's all a stunt, and the author refuses to give interviews or details."

"All right, that's all we can do from here. You've collected all of Smith's books, Kate?"

"Yes. The first three were out of print, but I managed to get them. Two copies of each book are in a leather satchel in the backseat of the car. When I could, I got them in large print."

I flinched a little at that. In reality, I hated searching for my reading glasses and large print made my life much easier.

Kate wouldn't let up. "As I've told you before, Flo, e-books are the way to go—you can adjust the size of the font."

"I want to hold books in my hands. We're moving into this nether world where nothing is real, and when it comes to books I put my foot down."

"Just as well," Kate said. "Only Smith's last one is even available as an e-book."

"Excellent. Then why are we having this discussion, Kate? We need our sleep. We'll head out at five, beat the morning rush hour."

"Really? Five am?" Kate asked. "We're making it a seven-day journey. Surely, we could start the day at a more decent hour."

"I'm happy to drive," I said. "I'm up at four, my usual cheerful self. You two can sleep in the car."

"Thanks, Flo, but I'll drive," Kate said. I could hear Maude let out the breath she'd been holding.

I smiled and headed off to bed. I knew Kate would never let me drive. Ever since I stopped in the middle of Fresh Pond Parkway in Boston because I missed a turn, Kate wouldn't let me near a main road.

THE DRIVE BEGAN in a most inauspicious way. No one spoke to me, which didn't bother me in the least. Marianne supplied us with coffee and doughnuts for the trip. The doughnuts were from Dunkin Donuts I'm quite sure. Maude had a pillow and blanket, and Kate was sullen—she always needed a strong cup of coffee and a couple of hours to welcome the day. I refrained from commenting on that. The less said the better.

We headed for Buffalo, our first overnight stop. Kate had a friend there that she hadn't seen in years—a man as I understood it. Maude and I would stay at the Curtiss Hotel so as not to cramp her style. Or mine. I believe in a good night's sleep always, but especially when one is on the road. I also require good work-out facilities. Kate was apparently willing to pass that up for the sake of some old boyfriend.

We'd barely left Boston when I heard Maude's breathy purr next to me. She could sleep standing up, I swear, or in this case, taking up two thirds of the backseat. I, on the other hand, had no need for excess sleep, so I pulled open the leather bag containing two copies of each of Smith's thirteen books.

The first was titled *A Taste for Murder.* The title sounded familiar, but I was quite sure I'd never read anything by this author. I asked Kate.

"Are you sure you don't mean *A Taste for Death* by P.D. James?" Kate said. "James wrote it in the '80s I think and it was nominated for a Booker. Adam Dalgliesh is the protagonist, and the murder takes place in a church. You probably saw the mini-series."

A few lights came on. "Yes, of course. I guess it's hard to find an original title for a piece of fiction. *A Taste for Murder* is the first book published by Smith."

I poked through the pile. "The second book is *The Name of the Lily*."

"*The Name of the Rose*," Kate said, "was a wonderful book. My mother loved it and insisted I read it. This is beginning to sound strange. What are the names of the rest?"

I pulled out two more. "*A Grand Delivery* and *A Thief in Time*."

"Sounds a lot like *A Grand Deliverance* by Elizabeth George and *A Thief of Time* by Tony Hillerman," Kate said. "Those were best sellers from the '80s. You can't copyright a title, so maybe Smith was hoping to cash in on the similarity of names. I wonder if it was only the title he or she chose to copy."

"I'll read the first one and let you know," I said. "Do you remember the plot of the book by P.D. James, Kate?"

"All I can recall is the murder scene—two men found with their throats slashed, one an alcoholic and the other someone who was titled. It was all very British."

I skimmed the opening of the book. "Our cowboy detective finds his way to an old Spanish mission and inside he finds two bodies—this time a man and a woman locked in a deadly embrace. No clue how they died."

"Sounds as if he borrowed but didn't outright steal the story," Kate said.

"Looks like it," I said. I settled back to skim the story and finished it before we stopped for lunch. I had to admit it was a good read.

Over lunch I gave them a summary. "Josh Logan, our protagonist, comes to LA in hopes of a movie career. It's the

1930s, and he's been told he has a good look and a perfect voice for the talkies. Cowboy pictures were popular in the thirties, and Josh can sing a bit. Coming from Texas and life on a ranch, he has the credentials to sound and look authentic. 'I can ride a horse, rope a cow,' he told the director of a new film. 'You won't need a stunt man, I can do it."

Maude sat across the table, munching on a salad, looking very content. She always liked a good story, and I could tell one. I'm not being boastful, it's simply always been one of my talents. Kate would say it's what helped me lie so convincingly, but even she nodded at me approvingly.

I took a few spoonfuls of my soup before it got cold. Then I continued.

"At first, it looked as if Josh had his future made. Then two things happened. When the lights went on and the camera started rolling for his screen test, Josh froze. Stage fright. Big time. The director said he'd give him one more chance the following day, but then the second thing happened. The director disappeared. Josh was desperate to find the guy because he could see his career going up in smoke.

"He found him all right. I already told you the scene. The director was locked in an embrace with a starlet, both dead. As it turns out they'd both been murdered. Some mysterious poison that knocked people off painlessly—they simply went to sleep and never woke up."

"Oh, my goodness," Maude said. "I'm on the edge of my seat. What happened? Were they lovers or did the murderer just make it look like they were?"

I smiled at Maude and finished my soup. Then I asked if we should get going.

"No hurry," Kate said. "We're only an hour or two outside Buffalo, so we have plenty of time."

I was a little disappointed to hear that. There is nothing

like leaving your readers, or in this case my listeners, with a cliff hanger.

"Very well, to answer your question, Maude, they were lovers. The starlet hoped to marry the director. The director seemed to have a number of young women he was stringing along."

"So there were lots of potential suspects," Kate said. "Another jealous starlet, a jilted lover. Nice."

"Dozens of possible murderers. It was a little difficult to keep them all straight. In the end it was a woman who had disguised herself as a make-up artist but was in fact the sister of the dead woman and the jilted lover of the director."

"Straight out of Agatha Christie," Kate said. "Poison and a murderer who is someone pretending to be someone else."

"Precisely," I said. "It seems our author doesn't like the idea of reinventing the wheel. He—or she—is content to borrow from other people's ideas."

"I wonder," said Maude, "if she got a little too close to someone's ideas and they decided to put an end to her."

"I see you are also convinced it's a woman."

"It would be consistent with how she writes," Kate said. "Disguise your identity with a pen name."

"Hmm. If she did steal her plots from others, that would certainly be a motive for murder," I said. "Maybe some poor soul didn't feel they were getting the credit they deserved."

"Yes," Kate said, "but why wait until her fame has evaporated. Why then?"

"Good question," I said, "to which we don't yet have a good answer."

We arrived in Buffalo early in the evening, and Maude and I spent a quiet night in the Curtiss Hotel. We agreed on a slightly later departure time of nine am to give Kate time to do whatever it was she had in mind with this long-lost friend of hers. She arrived in the morning a little after nine with a warm glow to her olive complexion.

"Nice night?" I asked.

"Definitely," Kate said.

End of story. Kate was always like that. She revealed nothing of her private life to me beyond assurances that she was quite happy with her single status. As was I. Never married and content to be so. Perhaps Kate and I were kindred souls in that respect, fiercely independent but never afraid of a good time. I suspect Kate's good times would make mine pale by comparison, but to Maude, we were both extraordinary adventurers.

"All right then. Off we go," I said.

We planned on lunch in Detroit and an overnight stay in Chicago. I pulled out the second book in Smith's series, *The Name of the Lily*. I had tried to read *The Name of the Rose* when it first came out, but I wasn't sure I'd actually made it through to the end. It was a little elaborate for my taste, but Kate was able to fill in the details of the original.

I was mainly intent on finding the death scene. There seemed to be a lot of them—by poison, drowning, bashed heads, fire, and a fall from high places. Which one, I wondered, had Smith been threatened with? Lily, as it turned out, was the name of the murderer.

Once again, it wasn't her true name. She, too, was in disguise. She was a vengeful movie critic who felt an actor had dumped her for his career. Here we were again—a person in disguise, like our author. Our author borrowed from the book with the similar name, but apparently not enough to get sued for plagiarism.

I was quite exhausted by the time we reached Detroit but curious to see how the city was faring. Such an earnest city in so much distress. We found pockets of renewal and ate lunch at Rose's Fine Food and dessert at Sister's Pie.

"I like this city," Maude said. "It reminds me of me. At one point seeming down and out but struggling hard to come back."

I smiled at Maude and swallowed my last bite of delicious cherry pie. "If this cherry pie is any indication, they might make it."

We climbed back in our car, and I was asleep in five minutes. I hate to admit it, but the pie and the temperature control in the back seat did me in. I woke to find us on the outskirts of Chicago.

The city with its glittering exterior and sense of robust good health was a sharp contrast to Detroit. We stayed at The Drake. My grandfather had been friends with the architects. My father took me one New Year's Eve to celebrate its 50th anniversary—1969 it was. I'd never been back since.

"You're joining us for dinner, Kate?" I asked. "No leftover boyfriend in this city?"

"Nope."

We settled into our separate rooms and spent the hour before dinner in blissful isolation. I did anyway. Togetherness is oversold.

Over dinner we discussed what we knew so far.

E. Elgin Smith was a decent writer. She got her plots from a variety of sources, and while her titles were knock-offs, her storyline seemed to have some originality to it. She used elements of plots from other books as a springboard for more outrageous ideas.

I skimmed book three, *A Grand Delivery*, during my hour before dinner while Maude tackled book number four, *A Thief in Time*. We chose the books which we'd read by the original authors to see what Smith stole and what she invented. I loved Elizabeth George and Maude had read every book written by Tony Hillerman.

"You first, Maude," I said after we'd ordered dinner.

"I haven't finished the book yet," she said. "I really love to read every word of a mystery, but I can tell you about the first deaths and the theme. In Hillerman's novel it's about ancient plots and history. Two men are found dead, one inside a truck, the other outside on some kind of ceremonial ground as I recall. I read that book a long time ago."

"And?" I asked. I tried not to sound impatient, just curious. Kate raised one eyebrow at me. "No rush," I added. "We have all night."

Kate frowned and sipped her martini. Maude knew me well enough to ignore my comments.

"In Smith's book, she talks about old artifacts from the silent movies," Maude said. "Clever adaptation, don't you think? Apparently the two victims had been bashed over the head with a candlestick from an old Bela Lugosi Dracula film. The candlesticks were missing."

"Hmm," I said. "In George's book, a young woman is found with an ax next to the decapitated head and body of her grandfather. Smith has a starlet with an ax standing over the slashed body of a producer, head missing. I get the feeling Smith isn't fond of men in Hollywood. They don't fare well. Was one of your victims a director or producer, Maude?"

"Yes!"

"Perhaps we have a clue here. Perhaps a producer or a director did Smith wrong. When was the first book written?"

"1990," Kate supplied. "All the books we've read so far had titles similar to best selling mysteries from the 1980s."

"So she does choose good books to use for her jumping off place," I said, "and she seems to care about well-written mysteries. Let's just speculate. Perhaps our Smith came to Hollywood in the late 1980s as an ingenue and some director or producer took advantage of her."

"There was plenty of that going around," Kate said. "One-way road to stardom. Could she have really been that naive?"

"Yes," Maude said. "Of course, she could. She probably thought if she was good enough, she'd make it on her merits and not who she slept with."

"Possible," I said. "Then she discovered that was not to be and took her revenge in a series of mysteries. I wonder if her descriptions of producers and directors match any who actually existed in Hollywood in the '80s. We'll have to check that out."

Our dinners arrived: a healthy kale salad for Kate, steak and pommes frites for me, and some chicken concoction for Maude. We set our speculations aside and enjoyed our meals.

We started in again over coffee.

"I'm still on the first book," Kate said, "but I love the cowboy detective Josh Logan. He's funny and charming like a cross between Jimmy Stewart and Clark Gable."

"He's just as wonderful in the book I'm reading," Maude said.

"So, is he based on someone Smith knew?" I asked. "He does come across as a star."

We'd covered about all we could with information we didn't have, so we called it a night.

The next morning, I expressed my concerns. "Our murderer has already tormented Smith through several would-be executions. I have this nagging concern we shouldn't wait many more days to get to LA. What if the murderer gets wind of our arrival date and decides to speed things up a bit?"

Kate looked over the itinerary. "We can drive eight hours today, skip our Des Moines stop and make it to Lincoln, Nebraska in time for dinner. The next day is a long drive anyway and takes us through Denver to Moab. Don't think we can change that one. Then I suppose we can drive through Las Vegas straight on to Los Angeles in a fourteen hour trip. I'm good with that if you two are. That would get us there in three more days instead of five."

"That would mean no gambling in Las Vegas, Kate," I said. "Can you handle that?"

"Very funny. I'm as tight with my money as you are with everything else."

"I assume that was meant to be an insult, Kate, but it missed its mark. Someone has to be in control, and I'm always happy to have it be me."

"We know," Kate said.

So, that was our new plan.

Kate drove, and Maude and I powered through the remaining nine books. Five of these had borrowed titles from the best of 1990 mysteries, and another two used best seller titles and modified death scenes from 2000. The last two titles we didn't recognize. The books were published annually until 2015. Nothing after that.

Each night, the three of us gathered over dinner to list the death scenes in the books we were reading. We had quite a long list. The last night before we were to arrive at the Huntley Hotel, we tried to make sense of it all.

"I wonder what Smith has gone through in terms of near-executions," Kate said.

We looked over our list. "That could be poison from the first book," I said. "Poison, drowning, bashed head, fire, and a fall from high places from the second one. No wonder I didn't love the original book, *The Name of the Rose.* Too much gratuitous violence. The third book, *A Grand Delivery* had a missing head. I wonder how our murderer would pull that one off as a near miss. And yours, Maude—two men bashed with a missing candlestick. It seems as if our tormentor must be nearly as clever as Smith herself."

"Yes," Maude said. "And who knows what's happened over the last several days?"

"You mean will we find her alive and in one piece?" I said.

"No reports of her murder," Kate said, scanning the LA Times. "She may be a has-been but she sold millions of copies in her time, so there would be a substantial obituary if she'd died."

"Yes, unless they haven't found her body yet," I said. "She may have become a recluse—many authors do. Still, someone may have been cleaning the house for her, taken care of her yard. Someone would have reported her death, surely."

That was it. That was all we had. We set out at five am that last morning and arrived at the Huntley at eight pm. Kate had made sure our rooms were available for our earlier arrival date. We ate a fast food dinner on the way and collapsed in our rooms for an early night, planning to meet at seven the next morning.

I was dead asleep when my bedside phone beeped to tell me I had a phone call. It was midnight.

"Thank God you picked up." I held the phone away from my ear. "Help me!" The person was shouting. A smoker's voice. Low and raspy.

"Who is this?"

"Smith. I'm Smith. He's doing it again. He gets closer each time."

"Are you safe?" I asked, now fully alert.

"I . . . I don't know." Muffled voices. "I'm up here," Smith shouted to someone. "Third floor."

There was shouting I couldn't make out.

I waited seconds that felt like hours.

"The police are here. I'm all right now."

I heard a crashing and splintering of something. More unintelligible shouts and then silence.

"Someone was trying to burn the house down with me in it. The police are handling it now. I'm safe for the moment."

"How did you know we were here?" I asked.

"Someone called me from the Huntley to say you were arriving early. Thank goodness for that! I'll see you as soon as I can get away from the police." Her voice which had sounded deep and raspy, was now more clearly female.

"So you are a woman," I said. "We thought as much."

"Yes, I'm a woman. At the Huntley I will be registered as Evelyn Jones." She must have looked at her watch. "I'm sorry to have awakened you. I was desperate and didn't think about the time. You get some sleep, you'll need it. I'll check in and come to your room around eight tomorrow morning. Will that suit you?"

"Anything will suit me."

She hung up without another word.

Could I possibly go back to sleep? When I thought of mansions burning, I thought of *Jane Eyre* and a wicked female villain. In *The Name of the Rose* the abbey was burned. These dramatic scenes usually happened toward the end of the book, so was our murderer making a mad dash to the finish line?

I let Maude sleep, but I knocked on Kate's door. She was awake and listened quietly as I told her what had happened.

"There isn't a lot we can do before she arrives," Kate said. "I could Google Evelyn Jones to see what pops up, but we have no reason to believe that's her real name. I think we have to wait and see what she has to say for herself in the morning."

"You're right, Kate. I can probably sleep now. We'll meet in my room at 7:30. I want you to rouse Maude in time. You seem to have a gentler touch than I do."

"You mean I don't blow that rooster blaring horn you think is so hysterical?"

"I packed light and didn't bring it."

I returned to my room, and I did sleep. I'm a practical person, and I realized if I didn't get my six and a half hours, I'd be no good to anyone. We all needed to be using every brain cell we had between us. At least we knew our potential victim was still alive.

SHE WAS PROMPT—I guess death threats can do that to a person—and she was not what I imagined, not in the least. But then what had I expected? She stood in the doorway of my hotel room, looking like a tiny mouse of a woman, dressed in a gray trench coat from the 1940s. Was this a joke?

She saw me studying her outfit. "I grabbed what I could find—something undamaged by the fire. A prop from a movie set."

I hadn't said one word, but she seemed to know what I was thinking. Useful for a writer.

"Please come in . . . Ms. Jones."

"Call me Evelyn—that is actually my name. My friends call me Evie—not that I have friends anymore. Once your fame evaporates, so do your friends."

I ushered her inside. Kate checked the corridor to make sure we had no unwelcome guests lurking about. No newspaper reporters. No murderers.

"All clear," Kate said, locking the door with the deadbolt.

"You came alone?" I asked.

"Yes. No fuss. No bother. I don't travel with an entourage. I never did."

I introduced her to Kate and Maude, each of whom shook her hand. I offered her coffee, which she accepted, and a cinnamon roll, which she declined. She settled on the sofa with Maude on one side and Kate on the other.

"What's your room number and do you have a bodyguard with you?" Kate asked.

"No bodyguard. If people need to reach me they can call me on my cell. I have no idea who I can trust."

"You should know your location is easily tracked with a cell phone. May I see it?"

Evelyn pulled it out of her pocket and handed it to Kate.

"I'll keep yours for now," Kate said. "Here, this is a disposable. I'm rerouting your numbers, so anything that comes through will go to us, and then we'll get in touch with you. All right with that?"

Evelyn took the new phone and shrugged. "It doesn't really matter what we do. He'll find me. He always does."

"You know it's a he?" I asked. "You have some idea of his identity?"

She shook her head. "I don't know any of that. I use 'he' in the old sense of the pronoun, not the new one. I have no idea what the sex of my murderer might be or the reason he or she wants to torture me."

"Really?" I asked.

She remained silent, sipping her coffee. We all studied her. She was more like a shadow than a living person. Gray hair, gray face without make-up, thin. Her whole body seemed to be withered, and yet I was quite sure she was considerably younger than Maude or me. In her sixties I would guess. A little old lady who could disappear into a crowd with nothing to make her remarkable.

She looked more resigned than frightened—*not* the way she'd sounded on the phone.

"I am not a very social person," she said. "I wasn't always this way, but circumstances have forced that on me."

"Circumstances?" I asked. "You mean the threats?"

She almost laughed, a dry 'ha' that finished in a smoker's cough. "No. My troubles started long before the death threats. I almost didn't write to you at all. The end of me might not be such a bad thing. It was the not knowing that I couldn't stand. I had to know who was doing this to me and why. That's why I wrote."

"You sounded frantic on the phone last night," I said.

"I'm embarrassed about that. I'd called the police and the fire department. No one seemed to be responding. That call was very unlike me. But I was trapped in a room with no windows, and a door that wouldn't open. I could smell the smoke. I panicked, and then the police finally came."

"Was the scene like something from one of your books?" Kate asked.

"It was."

"*The Name of the Lily*?" I said.

"No, my murderer has already used that book when he tried to bash me over the head. It was from a later book *The End Will Come.*"

"That one isn't a borrowed title," Maude said. "Normally, your titles are quite close to mystery best sellers. I hope I haven't offended you by saying that.'

"Not in the least. In the last years, I've grown tired of my games. I decided I could write without borrowing anything from anyone. I really thought I'd turned a corner, but the only corner I turned was to lose my readership. *The End Will Come* sold just well enough for me to get a contract for one more book. My last book *Death of a Spinster* barely sold a thousand copies. That meant I was dead to the publishing world."

"But you didn't lose your agent?" I said.

"Jeremy is a dear friend. He just put me on the bottom of his pile and encouraged me to keep writing, which I have."

"There is so much ground to cover," I said as I watched the sun stream into my window.

"Yes, and the first thing we must do is to try to throw your murderer off balance," Kate said. "He or she may know you're here, but they won't know more if you use the disposable phone and only call us with it. I'll keep your original phone."

"And I shall take your room," I said. "Where is it?"

"It's directly below this one," Evelyn said. "But I can't let you do that."

"Nonsense," I said. "However, directly below us may not give quick enough access to saving me from harm, should I need it. Do you know what your murderer might intend to do next?"

Evelyn shook her head. "As I said in my letter, he doesn't seem to go through the books chronologically, but he does seem to be picking up steam. The last two attempts were two days apart. If he were to go to my last book, then he would intend to push me off a balcony."

"Hmm. Most of these suites have balconies," I said. "Perhaps being downstairs will be all right. You'll hear a commotion, Kate, if he tries to push me over the railing, assuming he doesn't immediately see he's got the wrong person."

"Too many ifs for my liking," Kate said. "And yet I don't think we can involve the staff here. Information leaks out, no matter how discreet the staff may promise to be."

"It already has," I said. "Someone on staff called Evelyn to let her know we were coming early. Who was that?"

"A friend," Evelyn said. "Someone I trust completely."

"I should be the one pretending to be Evelyn," Maude said. "I have her same build and gray hair. You, Flo, would look more like a great brown bear pretending to be a kitten. You'd fool no one."

I looked at her. Maude did have the same general habitus. She was small and slim. "You'd be terrified," I said.

"No," Maude said. "I think I would be thrilled. A mystery turned into real-life drama. I'm not the despairing woman you found a few years ago. Or the one afraid of her own shadow." She turned to Evelyn. "I'm not sure I understand why you sound so resigned to your fate and the end of your life. Perhaps you'll tell us."

"It's a long story," Evelyn said.

"Over breakfast then," I said.

"I'd prefer that no one move into your room just now," Kate said, "until I have security worked out. Call no one but us on the new phone. You can text me anytime."

"Good. I don't want to talk with anyone anyway."

"Excellent." Kate said. "In the meantime, I'll let you know if anyone tries to contact you on your old phone and find out how you wish to respond."

It was nine before we had initial arrangements made. We'd leave Evelyn's room as it was, to suggest she might be coming back in a few moments. Kate would check it out for security and easy access to the floor above. I could imagine Kate developing a plan to swoop down from our balcony to Evelyn's should the need arise—just like in the movies.

By ten we were all getting antsy. By that, I mean I was antsy. "I've been cooped up in a car for five days," I said as the four of us sat down to a lunch Kate had fetched from a local restaurant. "I refuse to stay here waiting for something to happen."

"We could finish reading the books you wrote," Maude said to Evelyn. "Or you could summarize them for us. I enjoyed your second to the last one ,*The End Will Come.*"

"As that title foretold, the end will come. For all of us, won't it? My publisher went under immediately after that was published," Evelyn said. "It was the same time when a lot of publishers went out of business. The pressure of e-books and illiteracy I think."

Kate stared at her. "That sounds like something Flo would say—the illiteracy part. Are you as down on humanity as Flo seems to be at times?"

"I can't speak to that," Evelyn said. "But if Flo has mentioned we're going to hell in a hand basket, perhaps we are kindred souls. I came to Hollywood in the 1980s starry eyed. I was sixteen, claiming to be eighteen. I got a screen test right away. People said I looked and sounded like a young Katharine Hepburn. My hair was red in those days."

"I loved Katharine Hepburn," Maude said. "I still do."

"Well, it seems the director decided he didn't want a second Katharine Hepburn, particularly when I chose not to participate in his extra-curricular activities."

"You were too early for the #MeToo movement," Kate said. "Poor you."

"It wasn't so bad at first," Evelyn said. "I lived with other starlets, all of us jockeying for small walk-ons, some of us trying to do that without sleeping around."

I stood up, walked to the window and stared out at the beach, white and vast.

"It's not that I'm uninterested in your story, Evelyn. I suspect it holds the clue to who might want to see you dead. But I wonder if we might cover some ground as we talk. Literally. Could we visit your home, your stomping grounds? Have you always lived in Los Angeles?"

"I've lived in the same house in Santa Monica for almost forty years. It's still prime property although most buyers would tear down the house I have and start over. I don't have the money or interest in doing that. As I said I don't have many friends, so I don't entertain much. You are welcome to see my house—what there is left of it."

"We'll want you in disguise," Kate said. "I brought a few things at a local costume shop. See what you like."

Evelyn poked through two or three wigs. "These are very nice quality,' she said.

Kate smiled as if she'd used her own hair to make the wigs and had weaved them herself.

"This was the color of my hair when I was twenty," Evelyn said. "How does it look now?"

She held up a short, smart wig, rust colored and quite

gorgeous. I assumed she might look absurd in it, but she didn't. It took thirty years off her.

Kate saw me staring at the transformation. "Why don't you poke through these, Flo? You might like what you see."

"I'm perfectly happy with how I look, thank you very much." I edged closer to the pile and found Maude lifting out a silver gray wig that looked stunning with her fine features.

"Here," Maude said. "Try this." She handed me a wig that was a soft brown with streaks of gray. I took it into the bathroom where I could try it on undisturbed. As a younger woman I'd always been quite proud of my wavy brown hair, my best feature some boyfriends had told me. I'm sure Maude remembered that from our school days at Radcliffe and that's why she chose it for me. I slipped the wig on and felt myself fall back forty years. I kid you not. I still had my wrinkles but somehow my face or perhaps my new smile made all the difference. I walked out of the bathroom, and even Kate gasped.

"You look wonderful," she said. "We must go out on the town."

We snuck out the back way. Kate checked to make sure no one followed us. No one did. Our first stop was a champagne brunch Evelyn suggested at Fig in the Fairmont Hotel, not too far from her home. Then, properly relaxed, we ventured on to Evelyn's house.

It was not the most expensive house on the block, but it was in one of the nicest neighborhoods according to Kate. Ocean Park. Evelyn's house faced the ocean and was tucked behind a ten-foot gate. On either side of her were luxury condos.

She buzzed something, and the gate opened. Looking at the house from the outside, it was difficult to see that any damage had been done from the fire. Before we went inside, Kate walked the exterior to make sure no reporters or other strangers were lurking on the grounds. She took Evelyn's keys and searched the inside of the house as well. We waited until her return ten minutes later.

"All clear," she said.

Evelyn led the way. "The fire was the first attempt on my life that was made inside my house. I actually thought the murderer might not know where I lived. Now, I'm not sure I can come back to this."

It was a Mission style stucco house with a red roof and arched doorways. Evelyn led us through the tiled entryway to a curved staircase, and we followed her up the stairs to her office and bedroom on the second floor. It was in the hallway outside the office, that we saw the damage, mostly from smoke and water. The door to the office had been hacked through. Kate commented on how well the fire had been contained.

"The fire was meant to frighten me, not kill me," Evelyn responded. "The problem is I don't know when the dress rehearsals will be over and the final act will be played in earnest."

She showed us what the firemen had explained to her. The perpetrator used strips of material designed to give off smoke and some fire but also designed to self destruct within minutes. "It's the kind of stuff they use in movies," Evelyn said. "Even if the firemen hadn't come, I was in no real danger."

She must have seen the look on my face.

"I didn't know that, Flo. When I called you I thought I was about to die. Why would I have brought you out here if this was all a publicity stunt?"

I shook my head. "I can't imagine."

"Most of my neighbors don't know who I am. They keep to themselves, and I do the same."

"Why do you do that?" Maude asked as we walked back downstairs.

"I've been burned too many times—the upstairs notwithstanding. Every time I thought I could trust someone, I was mistaken. It was a lot easier to withdraw from the world and trust no one." She looked back at me. "Have you figured out about my books?" she asked.

I nodded slowly. "They're autobiographical aren't they, Evelyn?"

She smiled broadly at me. "Yes. I hoped you'd notice that. Each book has one element of truth—truth about my life—that I use to explain why a certain victim is chosen."

"So these are books of revenge," I said.

"I suppose you could say that," Evelyn said. "I've been wronged too many times to count."

We'd reached her spacious living room. "Sit down, and I'll fix you a drink." She pointed to a wall of plate glass windows and the sofa in front of it. "Sit over there where you can see the ocean." She fixed us each the drink of our choice.

For Kate and me it was a single malt scotch, so smooth we didn't speak for a few seconds. Maude had a California chardonnay, and Evelyn had water. "I don't drink much these days," she said. "I plan to be clear-eyed for my demise."

"You speak as if it's a fait accompli," Kate said, "and yet you have decorations up for Christmas." She nodded toward the grand tree in the center of the living room, the greenery that decorated the hearth and staircase. "It's very beautiful."

"Sometimes I can't sleep, like my mother. I spend the time productively, in this case decorating for the holidays. I hope to live through Christmas, my last Christmas, and I'm trying to enjoy the season."

I stood and looked at her hearth. "Three stockings?"

"Those are history from my childhood—two siblings and me."

"Are they still alive?" I asked.

"One is. A sister. We grew up in Minnesota. Sadly, my sister and I are . . . estranged."

"How estranged?" I asked.

"Not so much that she'd wish to torment or kill me," she said. "She blamed me for our brother's death— a skiing accident. Eric was my little brother, always following me. I skied down a harrowing slope, maybe to teach him a lesson. But he followed, like a fool, and broke his neck."

Evelyn spoke the words without any emotion, but I remembered reading in her first book about such a tragedy. Her young cowboy detective had lost his own brother—this one named Billy—in a cattle stampede. Josh blamed himself for the tragedy.

"You wove that into your first book," I said to her.

She nodded.

"It was very moving," I said.

"I found I could say in words what I couldn't seem to express in acting. Directors always said I was too wooden. But in my writing, my readers said they loved all the emotion, all the drama."

Kate looked at me. "What other autobiographical elements did you find in the books, Flo?"

Evelyn smiled. "Yes, Florence, I too would like to know what else you found."

"I haven't finished them all," I said, "but it did seem that each victim got what they deserved, and I wondered about that. You were always quite sympathetic to your murderers although they never got away with it. In the first books, the victims were directors or producers or fellow actors who were intent on taking advantage of some young woman. I suppose that was your experience in Hollywood."

"It was."

"Later there was a shift—"

A pounding on the front door made us all jump. Kate motioned us to be quiet, removed her gun from the inside pocket of her jacket, and approached the door. She looked through a peephole and turned back to us.

I'd never seen her look so perplexed.

"There's a woman standing on your doorstep who looks a lot like you, Evelyn. Would you care to explain?"

"Oh, dear. It's my sister, Emmy, I'm afraid."

"I thought you said you two were estranged," Maude said.

"That doesn't mean we never speak."

I stood and walked to the front door, peered through the peephole to see an agitated woman ringing the doorbell and shouting, "I know you're in there, Evie. Let me in this minute."

"She looks exactly like you," I said. "You didn't mention your estranged sister was your twin." I paused. "There was a twin sister in the third or fourth book. She'd been mistreated by a Hollywood agent, and for a while, it looked as if she might be a murderer."

Evelyn stood. "She is my identical twin, and she can be a troublemaker. I knew if I told you she was in town you'd think she had something to do with these pran—attempts on my life."

"You started to say pranks," I said. "You think this is all some elaborate practical joke?"

Evelyn did not respond as she walked slowly to the front door. She opened it, and Emmy slammed in like a tidal wave. "You look absurd in that wig! I know you heard me knocking. What's wrong with you? Are you deaf as well as senile?" She stopped when she saw the rest of us, but only for a moment. "What is this? Did you forget to invite me to some costume party? You all look ridiculous, I must add, with the exception of whoever you are. You must be their keeper."

"I'm Kate. And who are you exactly?"

"Take a good look. I'm Emma Catchem, Evie's sister."

We took a good look. She was Evelyn with make-up and hair that was expertly cut. Evelyn had removed her wig and we could see the same color hair—only hers was in a tangle. Evelyn was dressed in white, a long sleeveless sweater over a white sheath with a Hermes silk scarf draped around her neck. She looked chic, but that wasn't how she sounded.

"What have you done, Evie? Who is this motley crew? You contacted that bizarre group—old people protecting other old people. What a farce!"

"ODPA," I said. "Old Dames Protection Agency. I'm the president, Florence Wellington. And how do you know who we are?"

"Evie told me."

"I didn't," Evelyn protested.

"You stuck that letter in my face before you mailed it. I told you it was a waste of good money." She paused to take a breath. "The only person who could protect anyone is this young woman here, and that's because she has a gun."

Kate put her revolver away, and Emmy turned her venom on her sister once more.

"I told you this was someone who wanted to play with your head, and see—they succeeded. I don't know where you're getting the money for this group? It won't be from me."

"We come where we're needed," I said, "and work out the finances later."

Kate refrained from pointing out that to date our business had lost several thousand more dollars than it brought in, a hobby was how the IRS saw it.

"Do you think we could all sit down in this comfortable living room?" Maude asked, removing her wig.

"I came to speak to my sister, so I'll ask you all to leave." Emmy waved her hand toward the door as if we were some detritus she'd brought in on her shoes.

"They'll stay," Evelyn said. "They are my guests, and this is still my house."

"Not for long. Not with all your terrible financial investments. I've given you the last loan you'll get from me."

"I know that, Emmy. I won't ask you again. I thought perhaps we could bury the hatchet. Start over."

That remark seemed to leave Emmy speechless. But only for a moment. "What are you up to? Jeremy and I got your invitation for dinner at the Huntley tonight. What's that about?"

"I'm thinking of selling you my house. These threats have made me re-examine my life. I don't need all this space, and obviously I can't afford it."

"What?" Emmy said. "Have you had a stroke? Are you sick? You've never admitted defeat before."

"I'm not sick, but I am scared."

"I actually wondered if you were behind these so-called attempts on your life," Emmy said, "but why would you hire this crew if you were?" She stared hard at Evelyn. "We'll come tonight if you're serious about selling."

"I am. You look lovely in that outfit. Wear it tonight, won't you?"

"If you wish, Evie. I can't imagine what's come over you, but I'm willing to meet you halfway. I know Jeremy will be thrilled to get the property. We'll give you a fair offer."

Emmy exited, not as she'd entered. More like a tidal pool than a tsunami.

"You tamed the wild beast," I said to Evelyn.

She smiled. "I did, didn't I? It's probably time to sell, get me away from my would-be murderer. Lead a quiet life I can afford."

Maude nodded as if she were buying Evelyn's story.

I wasn't. "What is this all about?"

"I don't know what you mean?"

"You have a sister you hate who came here screaming at you. And now everything is sweetness and light."

"It will never be sweetness and light," Evelyn said. "Too

much has happened, but it's time to move on. It doesn't matter anymore."

"Doesn't matter?" I asked. "We're here to save your life— assuming this isn't simply someone messing with your head as Emmy suggests. It may be Emmy who wants to see you dead. You need to tell us about your relationship. with her"

"All right. If you must know, I'll tell you the whole sordid story on the back deck with another drink. Bundle up—it gets cold out there." She motioned to a pile of throws near the French doors that led to the outside. "I'm switching to Scotch."

We declined a second drink. I wanted to be alert as Evelyn told us what was really going on—starting with her sister. We heard the roar of the ocean as soon as we stepped outside onto the deck. The deck was walled on either side to provide privacy from the condos that abutted her property. A small path surrounded by oleanders lead from the deck to a beach.

Evelyn joined us with a Scotch in hand and a throw across her shoulders. "My sanctuary," she said, sweeping her hand across the vast Pacific ocean in front of us. "Here I can forget that anyone else in the world exists."

"Why would you want to do that?" Maude asked gently.

"Have you never wanted to escape the woes of the world, Ms. Merriwether?"

"Maude, please, and yes I have. But withdrawing from the world made me more miserable not less. Flo helped me realize that."

Evelyn turned to me. "So you're some kind of therapist along with being a detective?"

"No, no. No one would accuse me of being sensitive to other people's feelings. That's actually more Maude's talent. But why don't we start at the beginning—with your sister?"

We all settled into weathered teak furniture. Evelyn spoke loudly enough so that we could hear over the sound of the turbulent ocean.

"Emmy has always been a thorn in my side from the moment she was born. Before, most likely, wanting to take up my space and push me aside in the womb. It's always been like that. I was born first by six minutes, and Emmy never forgave me for that. We had none of that sister bonding you hear twins talk about."

Evelyn took another sip of Scotch. We waited.

"My brother died in the skiing accident as I said. He was ten and I was blamed for it. Before that, I was the golden child in the family—the best loved by both my parents. After he died, I became the pariah, the one who brought heartache to our happy home."

She finished off her Scotch in one giant gulp.

"It was never a happy home, actually. My mother was just this side of nuts. One minute she'd be all gloom and doom, in the bed, lights off. The next she'd be repainting our dining room. She drank morning to night. She'd go off to a mental hospital when things became too much for her—I think my father sent her there when she needed to dry out. Mother expected us girls to live the glamorous life she never had. I was sixteen when my brother died and everyone turned on me. It was my chance to escape from expectations gone sour and from my sister."

"Yet here she is," Maude said.

Evelyn gave her a bitter smile.

"Emmy couldn't let go of me, for whatever reason. She followed me to Hollywood, said we could be a sister act. She'd watched *White Christmas* a hundred times. She was convinced we could be Rosemary Clooney and Vera-Ellen, despite the fact neither one of us could sing or dance.

"We spent three miserable years together in a tiny studio apartment, glued at the hip, auditioning for all the same parts and getting rejected. Then Emmy chose a different path. What was wrong with sleeping with a few people along the way? Everyone did it. I was foolish to be such a prude."

Evelyn stood and entered the house with no explanation. She returned with another Scotch, this time a double.

"Emmy got some two-bit parts in B grade movies. We parted ways at that point. She moved in with one boyfriend or another until they grew tired of her. Then she'd stay with me for a month or so, until she found a new patsy."

"Sounds like you think she was taking advantage of people," Maude said, "not the other way around. But you were both so young. Teenagers really."

"I saw the truth, but a lot of other people took her side. My family for one. Poor Emmy. Never gets a break. I'd known Emmy all my life. She was a user and that never changed."

"You seem to hate her a great deal," I said, "and yet you say you want to bury the hatchet, sell her the house you love."

"I'd say I'm disgusted with her, but I can't afford this house any longer. I can't even pay my real estate taxes. My attacker knows where I live. It's time to go."

"You were telling us about your sister," Maude said gently.

"After a few years in Hollywood, I turned to writing and Emmy kept trying to be an ingenue—long after she was too old for that role. Finally, she managed to catch a big fish. Not a producer or a director, but someone with money. Someone who was willing to back pictures in which she could star. They were flops, all of them. Emmy gave up on acting and married the guy, Douglas Catchem, thirty years her senior. He died two years later and left her a very wealthy woman."

"Anything suspicious about his death?" I asked.

Evelyn looked at me as if I knew something I didn't. "He was an old man, overweight, taking all kinds of medicines. He died on the tennis court. Heart attack. Emmy was on the court when it happened, and she said he died instantly. So, do I think she might have done something to hasten his death or even cause it? I wouldn't put it past her. I wouldn't put anything past her."

"Yet, you don't think she's involved with these attempts on your life," I said. "Why not?"

"Emmy has nothing to gain from my death. She's a wealthy woman, and it's likely she'll soon own *this* house. I paid for the house outright when I was a bestseller, but I've had to borrow money to keep living here. I got bad financial advice like a lot of people in Hollywood. If Emmy wants this 'perfect location', I've decided I'll sell it to her."

"You don't think she'd kill you for it?" I asked.

"She wouldn't get it that way," Evelyn said. This time she laughed outright. "I have a will that leaves it to a writers' charity, and she's aware of that. Her goal is to keep me alive, not kill me. She came here to make sure I was still kicking. You can see how pleased she was at the thought I might sell."

"And will you?" Maude asked. "Did you mean what you said?"

"I haven't made up my mind about that. I'll see how I feel this evening. It would mean my sister had won. Again."

I was beginning to get cold. Not just from the wind but from Evelyn's change of heart.

"I think it's time to go inside," I said.

"Of course," Evelyn said. She led us into the living room.

Kate glanced at her watch. "We should get back to the hotel—before it gets dark, and we can't see who might be lingering outside."

"Has the murderer ever struck twice in the same place?" Maude asked. "In your books, the ones I've read, your locales are always different."

"You are as observant as Florence," Evelyn said. "My murderer has never struck in the same place twice. He's not likely to come after me here."

"Then perhaps we should just stay here," Maude said,

"and figure out who the person is who wants you dead before he strikes again." She'd wrapped herself in a throw and settled on a cushy overstuffed sofa.

"It's a thought," Kate said. "I could turn this place into a fortress without too much trouble."

"No," Evelyn said. "I've paid for the rooms at the Huntley, and I have the dinner party planned there."

"How could you afford to pay for all that?" I asked. "You seem to have very little money from what you say."

"I know one of the managers—she's the one who called me about your early arrival. She loves my books, so she practically gave the rooms to me. As to the dinner, I assume Emmy will pick up the tab if I agree to sell the house."

"This isn't good news about the rooms, Evelyn," Kate said. "It means at least one person knows you're staying there, and probably she also knows that we're there to protect you."

"She'd never tell a soul," Evelyn protested.

"Most people love to gossip," I said. "I suspect the cat is out of the bag, but it can't be helped. Now what?"

"Didn't the murder in your last book, *Death of a Spinster,* happen in a hotel like the Huntley?" Maude asked.

"Yes, it did. My protagonist, Josh Logan, falls in love. He's older now, done with sowing his wild oats. He meets a quiet librarian type on holiday at an oceanside resort. That unfortunate woman is murdered and Josh is convicted of the crime."

I was beginning to smell a rat.

"Evelyn, what's going on?" I asked. "Why are you so determined we stay at the Huntley?"

"I want this over," she said. "I've already written the final story for my cowboy detective. It will be released posthumously —if I should die. Jeremy has promised that if anything happens to me, he'll make sure it sees the light of day. I will be famous once more."

"I need another Scotch," I said and made my way to the bar. "Anyone else?"

Kate shook her head. "One of us needs to be stone-cold sober."

"Make that two of us," Maude said.

I poured a small Scotch for myself and didn't offer another one to Evelyn. "How does the spinster die?" I asked.

"That's really the best part," she said. "It appears she's been thrown over a balcony by my cowboy detective no less. He's arrested and winds up going to jail for a murder he didn't commit."

"That's how your story ends?" I asked. "No wonder it didn't sell well."

Evelyn laughed. "You're right of course. I knew my readers would be upset, but it isn't as if I killed Josh off. I just stuck him in jail. He was convicted of manslaughter, so my readers could believe he'd get out in a few years."

"And does he?" I asked. "In this secret sequel of yours does he manage to get out?"

"It's much more complicated than that," Evelyn said. "This final book is really my masterpiece. It reveals what actually happened in *Death of a Spinster*—the truth behind the story."

"And yet, you don't plan to be alive to see it published," I said.

Again she laughed. I wasn't really enjoying the change in Evelyn's behavior. She was sounding slightly maniacal.

"I shouldn't have had that second Scotch," she said. "Everyone will believe I'm dead, that's certain."

"What is your plan, Evelyn?" This time it was Maude who asked.

"My plan is to go out in a blaze of glory if that's necessary. It will be a grand dinner party tonight. My sister will be there, my agent, Jeremy—faithful to the end—and of course the three of you. The restaurant is lovely, on the 18th floor, with an open balcony. If my murderer chooses to strike there I'll be available. Perhaps, you'll save my life, Florence, as you claim you are talented at doing. ODPA, such a quaint name for a group of women well past their prime. We'll see, won't we?"

We all stared at her, and I think she realized she'd let her mask fall away more than she intended.

"I meant nothing bad by that statement. I too am past my prime or so everyone tells me. We'll all be fine tonight with any luck."

I sank into the soft sofa next to Maude. I needed to think.

"It seems Emmy mentioned Jeremy as if they were close. Is that your agent, Jeremy Lambert? Were you and he ever an item?"

Evelyn giggled. Another strange response.

"You've been reading old tabloids, haven't you, Flo? Clever of you. We were an item as you say in your antiquated way."

"What happened?"

"I grew tired of him, especially when he could no longer find me a publisher."

"So you dumped him?"

"You sound as if you don't believe me. Yes, I dumped him. Emmy picked up the pieces as she has done before with someone else I once loved."

"Who was that?" I asked.

"Why do you care?" Evelyn moved slowly to a chair and sat down. "I don't have to say another thing to you."

"We came at your request," I said. "I now realize it was most likely under false pretenses. I'm going to find out about it one way or another."

"You still work for me. You'll do what I want you to do. You'll get a story out of it—one you can put on your Facebook page. Maybe you'll prevent a murder, who knows? Anyway, you'll see it all unfold. Tonight. On schedule."

"I think not," I said. "Kate, do you have the agent's number?"

"Yes. Tell him we need him here as soon as possible. It's a matter of life and death."

"This is outrageous," Evelyn said. "This is my house, and you are in my employ. I want you out now."

Hmm, she had a point. I wondered what we could do legally.

Maude spoke up. "In a situation in which we think someone may be about to commit a crime or be a danger to themselves or someone else, can't we make a citizen's arrest?"

She looked at Kate, but I responded.

"Yes, Maude, we can," I said. One of my great strengths was to sound convincing even when I didn't know what I was talking about. "We can confine you to your house, Evelyn, and that's what we'll do."

Evelyn stood. "I'm calling the police."

"By all means. I'd like them here," I said. "Of course, they may need to arrest you, but that's your call."

"I've done nothing wrong," she said.

"Oh no?" Kate asked. "When I checked out the house, I looked over the smoke and fire damage outside your bedroom. You were never at risk of harm."

"I didn't know that at the time," Evelyn said.

"I think you did," Kate said. "You got a little sloppy about things—I found more of the material that was meant to look dramatic and cause no harm. I found it in your garage."

"I suppose you think you caught me red-handed. My handyman was supposed to dispose of that," she said.

"He didn't apparently."

"You completely misunderstand me," Evelyn said. "My life was at risk, and I couldn't seem to get the attention of the police. I needed to show them just how desperate things were."

"Which is why you called me," I said, "in the middle of the

night. You are a good actress, Evelyn. I believed you. But I don't believe you now. Kate, can you track down her sister as well as her agent?"

"Probably."

"I think we need to hear Emmy's side of things."

"She'll lie the way she always lies," Evelyn said.

"Then why, may I ask, would you have her attend a dinner this evening?"

Evelyn was quiet for a moment and then turned on me, chin out, eyes narrowed.

"She's the victor once more, and I decided to acknowledge it. She can have the house. I plan to go away."

"Did she win in terms of your love life as well?"

Evelyn looked at me as if I were indeed an amazing detective. While I loved the idea of that, Kate had actually found a description of E. Elgin Smith on Wikipedia. He was described as someone who had a brief but disappointing relationship with a Douglas Catchem, big in the tech industry. After it, Elgin Smith went into seclusion. The article implied it was a homosexual relationship, but I recalled that her sister's last name was Catchem.

I couldn't resist. "Douglas Catchem," I said. "I guess you didn't catch him or couldn't keep him. I assume he chose your sister over you and left her with a fortune when he died."

"He loved me first. He was about to marry me, and then she came along and destroyed my happiness, the way she always did. You are as cruel as she is."

Evelyn rose, grabbed a brass-handled poker from the fireplace set, and rushed at me. Maude stuck her foot out and Kate grabbed the poker from her hand before she fell at my feet.

"Now, I think we really *can* make a citizen's arrest," I said.

Kate placed Evelyn in a chair across the room from us and ordered her to stay put. She called the agent and the sister who agreed to meet at Evelyn's house. Then she called the police.

"Do you want to tell us what's going on?" I asked. "Or do you want me to tell you?"

Evelyn sneered, her transformation complete. "Be my guest."

"I think you planned to bury the hatchet tonight—into the back of your sister. I'm not sure how you intended to make that happen with so many witnesses, but I do think you meant to use us as dupes. We would be there validating your innocence."

Evelyn stared straight ahead and said nothing.

"The next book, your final book, must be somewhere," I said. "On some computer, locked away in the house. That should tell us all we want to know."

I looked at Kate and Maude. We stood as one. "Rock, scissors, paper," I said to see which one of us would guard Evelyn.

"That's nonsense," Kate said. "I'm the only one strong enough to take care of Evelyn if she decides to act up. I'll wait here and let our guests in when they arrive."

I watched Evelyn's eyes as we searched the downstairs for the usual hiding places. Kate pointed out it could be on a thumb drive. Heading to the kitchen, I saw Evelyn smile slightly—not there. She smiled again when I veered into the downstairs den. She stopped smiling when Maude and I headed upstairs.

She rose as if to follow us, and Kate pushed her back into her chair, a little roughly. It didn't take us long. I doubt that Evelyn expected anyone to search her house for some secret manuscript. No one would imagine it would be the plot for the perfect murder.

We didn't find it on the computer in her office. We searched her bedroom. In the closet was a white sheath and sweater that matched what Emmy had been wearing earlier. And what Evelyn had asked her to wear again that evening.

Under the mattress, we found the manuscript. Hand written, in the same beautiful script she used when she requested our help. She'd taken her time, apparently feeling she was in no hurry to end the story, possibly her last story.

We came down to the living room—I let Maude carry the manuscript—and we watched Evelyn's face crumble. "You can't do this to me," she screamed. "You can't rip this away from me. My sister set you up to do this, didn't she? Somehow, she figured out what I was going to do."

The doorbell rang before I could respond. Jeremy arrived with Emmy. They looked as if they were a couple, and I wondered if that was the final blow for Evelyn.

"You know, don't you?" Evelyn said to them. "You know all about it."

They gave her a blank look.

Emmy spoke first. "What are you talking about? You've canceled the dinner party for tonight? As if we care. I never believed you wanted to make amends, but I was curious about what you were up to. That devious mind of yours has always intrigued me."

"*My* devious mind?" Evelyn exploded. "You've taken everything from me that I've ever wanted. And you started with our brother. It was you on the slopes taunting him to be brave and ski down that impossible mountain. You killed him and blamed it on me."

Emmy didn't deny it.

"You followed me to Hollywood so you could torment me."

"I followed you because I thought you might make something of yourself. I thought we might soar to the heights with a sister act. That's why I came. That and the fact that our parents began to suspect I might be behind the accident that killed Eric."

I watched as Jeremy disengaged himself from Emmy. He stood to one side and listened.

"What drove you to this, Evelyn?" I asked.

I took the book from Maude and began to thumb through it. "I'm sure it's all in here somewhere. The last broken relationship. The final one your sister stole from you." I looked at Jeremy standing a few feet from everyone. "You said you broke off the relationship with your agent, but perhaps it was the other way around."

"Of course it was," Emmy said. "Evelyn could never keep a man. She was a cold fish, always thinking of herself."

"Two peas in a pod," I said. "You could be describing yourself, I suspect."

"Finally, someone has your number," Evelyn said. She seemed to perk up a bit. She turned to me. "She uses everyone, most of all me. And I've had enough. When Jeremy said he was through with me, I knew I was done with the lot of them.

"I loved him. Jeremy was part of the inspiration for my cowboy detective Josh Logan. My brother Eric was the other part. One dead and the other now, as good as dead to me. It was time to end the story and get rid of the lot of them."

"Police," someone shouted from outside. "Open up."

Kate went to the door and let in a lone policeman.

"What is it this time? Another fire?"

"A confession," I said. I introduced myself and the others in the room and suggested the officer—Officer Gallagher as it turned out—take a seat.

"A confession?" Officer Gallagher asked. "Do you wish to make a statement, Ms. Jones, or do you want to speak to a lawyer first?"

"I'll talk. All I want now is peace."

Officer Gallagher read her her rights.

"It's all in the book, anyway. It was a simple plan—a murder in front of everyone. I convinced Emmy she could finally have the property. I'd hand it over officially at a dinner tonight at the Huntley. I invited Jeremy to come as well. A kind of launch party I told him for my final book."

She looked at the two of them seated on opposite ends of a long couch. "He thought I didn't know about his relationship with Emmy. Emmy made sure I knew little details meant to torture me. At first, they did. But after so many disappointments, a new one is simply another notch in the belt of a disappointing life."

"You knew I was going to help you get this last book published," Jeremy said. "You knew you could count on me."

"Jeremy, you're such a fool. I could see what Emmy was doing to you. You've always been so weak."

"And you, sister dear, have always been a woman who breaks a man's spirit," Emmy said. "That's what you did to poor Jeremy and what you tried to do with Douglas Catchem. It wasn't that I stole him away from you. He was anxious to leave. I know how to treat a man."

"You know how to manipulate them," Evelyn said. "I'll give you that. I was the one with talent—you were the one who could convince people to do what you wanted them to do. But all that was going to end."

Officer Gallagher thumped the incident report on his clipboard. "I'm not here to listen to squabbles between family members. I can do that at home."

"You're impatient like every man I've ever known," Evelyn said. "Very well. We'll get on with it. Perhaps, Flo, you'd like to read from page 307. I believe my handwriting is legible enough. I'll set the stage for you. Josh had plenty of time to think in prison, and that's what he did. He went over and over the murder scene until he finally understood it."

I turned to the page. It was the last chapter.

"The hotel had outdone itself. Christmas in full array with a silver-decorated tree in every free space. Ellen's only requirement had been a dining table with access to the balcony. Josh wasn't sure why she wanted that or what the dinner was all about. He was fond of Ellen, not sure he could say he loved her yet, but that might happen. Josh was ready to give up his life of near-death experiences in Hollywood. He'd been beaten to within an inch of his life, shot at and occasionally wounded. So what if she was five years older? He was no longer the prime specimen he'd once been."

Officer Gallagher sighed loudly. "Is all this really necessary?"

"Very necessary," Evelyn replied. "You do realize what you're hearing, I hope. I write as E. Elgin Smith, and this is the last book in my Joshua Logan Cowboy Detective series."

Gallagher looked up at her. "But that author was a guy. I loved those books, and so did my mother. I assumed Smith must have died. You're telling me you wrote those?"

"If you listen to the writing, Officer," I said, "you'll recognize the style."

Gallagher put his clipboard down and settled back on the sofa. I kept reading.

"Josh dressed carefully for the dinner. Formal, Ellen had said, so he left his cowboy hat and boots at home. With luck he'd see Ellen's sister there. Elizabeth. They were twins, but she had something Ellen lacked—a kind of lust for life. She'd be fun in bed, he speculated. She was also a very wealthy widow. Maybe he was involved with the wrong sister. Maybe he could sort that out before things went any further.

"It was a small gathering. The two sisters and Josh. Something about it made Josh a little nervous. Ellen fussed over her sister, which seemed unnatural. From what he knew, Ellen wasn't a big fan of Elizabeth. Ellen said she had a major announcement to make, and her sister asked her to get on with it. They began bickering as sisters will do.

"At first Josh simply listened or tried not to listen, but things got more heated. Other people in the dining room turned to look at them. Josh, ever the good person, tried to quiet them. 'Stay out of this, Josh,' Ellen ordered. 'You're disturbing the other guests,' Josh said quietly. 'You always care so much about what other people think,' Ellen said, 'and so rarely about me. We'll take it outside so we won't disturb you or the steak you ordered.'

"Ellen virtually dragged Elizabeth to the balcony. She closed the glass door, but Josh could still hear their voices, now muffled but angry. Then he heard a scream. He lurched for the door and got to the railing outside in time to see one sister push the other over the balcony to the street eight stories below. He grabbed the remaining sister, not sure at first who it was.

'You pushed her,' he said. 'I saw you.'

'I tried to stop her from killing herself.' It was Ellen—at least he thought it was Ellen. In the darkness of the balcony he couldn't say for sure. They were identical twins, and perhaps it was Elizabeth, but no—he recognized the scarf around her neck as a gift he'd given Ellen for Christmas.

'She thought you and I were having an affair.'

'Who are you? You're wearing Ellen's scarf.'

'She gave it to me at dinner, said it no longer meant anything to her. You don't remember that? Oh my God, Josh, you don't even recognize me? I'm the woman you're meant to be with— Elizabeth, of course.'

She threw her arms around Josh, and at first he responded, but a moment later he recoiled. 'No,' he said. 'I saw what you did. I'm calling the police.'

'It will be your word against mine,' she said. 'A brute of a man, who threw a small woman over the balcony.'"

I took a breath. "Shall I read more?" I asked. Everyone nodded.

"Let me skim a bit," I said.

Evelyn was not pleased.

"Give it to me. I'll read the important parts."

She turned to the next page and started to read.

"The trial was a short one. Fellow guests had witnessed Josh's rush onto the balcony. They'd heard banging against the balcony and then a second scream. It all made sense. Josh, a big man, had pushed a small woman to her death. Someone who might stand in the way of his marrying a very wealthy woman for her money. He got ten years. Elizabeth, or was it Ellen, looked on sadly during the trial and wrote to Josh his first years in jail. He never returned the letters and finally she stopped writing. The police never knew who had actually been killed. This was due to a unique malformation the women had —no fingerprints. It was a long-standing malady in the family that affected the women only and was a blessing or a curse depending on how you looked at it."

Evelyn closed the book.

Officer Gallagher sat up. "You still have it," he said with a sigh. "I can't wait to read the whole thing."

"It's a confession!" I yelled at him. "She's confessing to what she planned to do this evening. Don't you understand that?"

"But, she hasn't done any of it, has she?" Officer Gallagher said. "What do you want me to arrest her for? Wishful thinking?"

He smirked and stood up to leave.

"You can arrest her for attacking Florence Wellington," Kate said. "She was about to hit her with a fireplace iron. We all witnessed it."

The officer sat down again. "You sure you want to do this?"

"Quite sure," I said. I didn't like being played for a fool.

"You do realize you won't be getting a fee for your services," Evelyn said. "And when this comes out you and your agency will look ridiculous."

"I never expected to see that fee, and I'm quite happy with

the results. We saved at least one life whether the police believe that or not. I'm quite sure the newspapers and our blog readers will be happy to hear the truth."

"I have a question," Maude said, "about the fingerprints. Is any of that true?"

Evelyn and Emmy held up their hands. "Quite true. No fingerprints. A rare genetic disorder called adermatoglyphia," Evelyn said.

"Since we've moved onto trivia," I said, " I have a question for you—why does everyone's name start with an 'E' in your extraordinary family?"

"You've already answered it, Florence," Evelyn said. "Mother stated that all her children would be extraordinary— only the word she used was 'exceptional.' She didn't want us to forget that; therefore every one of our names had to start with E. I used it in my pen name. A double dose. I was sure it couldn't hurt."

Evelyn seemed to be delighted with how everything turned out. I asked her about that.

She grinned. "I'll sue you of course for libel if you accuse me of being a would-be murderer, and that will make my book a bestseller. I'll be on top again, and maybe I'll have my protagonist get out of jail in time for another book. E. Elgin Smith rides again and perhaps Josh Logan will as well."

She held her hands out to Officer Gallagher, apparently waiting for him to handcuff her. "I'll go quietly. I'll be out in a few months if they even prosecute the case," she said to me. "Jail will be a nice place to work on my next book, give it lots of authenticity."

She had indeed outfoxed me, and I hated that.

"I'm done," I said to Kate and Maude. "Let's get out of here."

Emmy stopped me on the way out. "I'll pick up the tab for you at the Huntley—my sister would have left you holding the bag for all of it. Enjoy a dinner on me. In fact, I'll pay all your expenses for the trip."

I nodded. I couldn't get a thank you out of my mouth.

"You saved my life," she said.

"I hope so."

Honestly, I wasn't sure both sisters would survive, and I wasn't at all certain who might do the other in. But, it wasn't my concern any longer.

Kate, Maude and I went back to our rooms at the Huntley. We enjoyed one more night there and had a lovely dinner on Emmy's tab. Kate lifted a glass of the Huntley's finest champagne as we lingered over dessert. "We have reason to celebrate. If Emmy does as she promises, we will more than break even this year. We'll see a profit."

"I'll drink to that," I said.

Maude joined in. "Congratulations, Flo. I always knew you'd make a go of it. I loved this adventure—with just the right amount of danger. And now we can relax."

At that moment, our waiter approached and asked if he could get us anything else. He had a lovely Texas drawl, and I took a good look at him. Apparently, Kate and Maude had the same thought I did. He was gorgeous.

"I apologize, ladies. Y'all don't know me; I just came on. Finished a local theater production. Name's Josh."

"I suppose it's Josh Logan," Maude said with a laugh.

"Yes, ma'am, it is. How'd you come to know that?"

Kate leaned over to me. "He looks exactly the way I imagined Josh would look from the books. Jimmy Stewart reincarnated."

He must have heard. "Ladies, I reckon you caught me out. Josh Logan is my stage name. I grew up on the E. Elgin Smith books, came to Hollywood because of them. I sure hope I don't end up like that other Josh Logan—locked up in jail for a murder I didn't commit."

He left, and a little shiver ran through me. "You think Evelyn set up that last encounter? To make sure we knew she might still be around?"

"Or maybe it was Emmy," Kate said.

The breeze from the balcony, which had previously felt refreshing, now had a cold, hard edge to it. None of us considered going out there. Who knew where one of those sisters might be lurking?

THE END

4

MRS. CLAUS AND THE LITTLEST REINDEER

K ate couldn't stop laughing. I finally had to send her out of the room. No doubt she was headed for Natalie, our housekeeper, who walked around the house with a duster in one hand, so she could pretend to be busy if I bumped into her during the day.

At this moment, I heard Natalie in the main parlor calling on ECHO for some Zumba tunes.

"Nothing better than a little dance music when one is straightening up," she liked to tell me. Straightening up was the term she used when she had nothing to do and could watch TV or dance the day away unless I happened to enter the room. Then she straightened up.

They were two peas in a pod. You almost never needed either one of them, but when you did, well, you really couldn't do without them.

Like Kate, my so-called bodyguard, Natalie would think it

was a hoot that I was being asked to play the part of Mrs. Claus. That's what she'd say—I could hear it. "Isn't that a hoot? Type casting—not." Then they'd snort together, whooping and hollering until I found them and told them they were both fired.

None of that would faze them, and it wouldn't help my current situation.

Maude asked if I was going to do it.

"Really, you expect me to wear a costume as if I were going to some ghastly Halloween party?"

"I just don't see how you can get out of it. Miles Tanner was your father's oldest friend. Now, he's the last man standing from that group of movers and shakers. You told him you'd do anything in the world for him."

"Stop, Maude. He's hardly standing these days. I told him he needed to work on his posture years ago, and now it's too late."

I stared at myself in the pier mirror that stood in our entrance hallway. I looked dignified with excellent posture. I didn't slouch, never slouched, and still stood over six feet tall. Hadn't lost an inch. My personal trainer, Penelope, was very proud of me. She wouldn't think it was hilarious that someone wanted me to play Mrs. Claus. She'd think it was an outrage.

Maude, always sympathetic, asked what I was going to do.

"Perhaps I'll come down with something," I said.

Maude smiled at me. "You've never been sick a day in your life and you don't lie—unless it's absolutely necessary and never to your friends."

She had a point.

"Miles is a sweet old man," I said. "I'll think of something."

Kate came back into the room.

"I'm sorry, Flo," she said. "It's just the whole idea is so hysterical. You and Mr. Tanner, Santa and Mrs. Claus for the

Aim High benefit. Actually, I think you should be flattered. It's your favorite non-profit, and he could have asked any number of California celebrities. Instead, he chose you."

"I do love the cause," I said.

Maude gave me a questioning look. "Aim High?"

"Aim High helps middle-school children in northern California prepare for life and higher education. I've visited their summer program and they are very impressive. I'm glad they're finding support out of state. Miles is from California, went to school in Berkeley before he moved east. He's never forgotten his roots."

"Why did Miles choose you?" Maude asked. "When you know . . . he could have asked Meryl Streep or Judi Dench. Maggie Smith would have done it in a heartbeat."

"Is that supposed to make me feel better?"

Still, it was a good question. Why did Miles insist it be me? He said he'd explain over tea in the Map Room Tea Lounge, part of the Boston Public Library. He knew I loved that tea room surrounded by books, and somehow, he thought I'd jump at the chance to attend his grand Christmas Eve celebration in full regalia.

"NOT MUCH NEED FOR PADDING, FLO," he joked when I arrived at his table and he flung his arms around me.

"I'm a big woman, Miles, but I have not gone to fat, not like some people I could mention."

I poked him in the ribs.

"Quite right, Flo. I'll be the perfect Santa except for the fake beard."

The sound of his laugh was music to my ears. I hadn't seen Miles much since my father's death ten years earlier, but the ring of his laughter brought everything back to me. I recalled my father sitting in our library with Miles beside him, a roaring fire in front of them and good brandy in snifters. They would talk for hours and laugh uproariously over Miles's exploits.

Sometimes I would listen in, pretending to read a book in the back corner of the library. Miles was a storyteller, so it was impossible to know which part of his adventures were true and which were exaggerated. Father would often add his own exclamations—"That can't be true" or "You didn't."

And Miles would always respond, "Of course, it's true. Would I lie to you, John?"

For a moment I basked in the warmth of those memories.

Miles ordered tea and a scone for me. He waited until the food arrived and I'd had my first sip of tea.

"I don't like to bring you into this, Flo," he said. "Your father would be appalled to think I was putting you at risk."

Now, my ears perked up.

"Really, Miles, my father taught me to go where I was needed. Always. What's wrong?"

"I'm not sure that anything is wrong, but it might be. You see, a few days ago I got wind of a plot against my life."

I squeezed his hand. "That's hardly nothing, Miles."

He smiled at me and covered my hand with his. "Flo, if I were ten years younger . . ."

"Enough of that," I said and pulled my hand back to sip my tea. "Father warned me about you when I was an innocent teenager. Let's get back to the matter at hand."

"It's just possible my romantic exploits are part of this whole thing. They may have come back to haunt me."

"What?"

"This may shock you, Flo."

"Almost nothing shocks me, Miles. You know that, and I'm far from a prude. Out with it."

"I'm a scrupulous man, in my own way. Like you, I never married. Didn't seem fair to any wife I might have. I knew I was not the type to settle down permanently with one woman. I've had a number of what I'd call serial relationships. Normally, one at a time, sometimes for years. And, here's the important part, sometimes with offspring."

"Ahh."

"Yes, ahh. I always warned the women that I didn't make good marriage or father material, but if it happened I promised I would make sure the children were taken care of until they reached their majority."

"And there were offspring?"

"A few."

"You sound proud of that."

"I suppose I am—honestly, I didn't know I had it in me."

"But a child needs a father. You had a father."

"I had a rogue for a father. I didn't want to be like him. I'm glad to say that most of the children I produced grew up in happy homes, just not *my* home."

"Really, Miles!"

"You see, I have shocked you."

"You didn't shock me. Disappointed me, perhaps. You've always seemed to me to be a kind and considerate man. This sounds neither."

"Apparently, someone else agrees with you."

So this was why Miles suddenly wanted me at his side. "Someone is threatening you?"

"It's not exactly a direct threat—more an indication of what might happen to me in the future."

"You've lost me," I said.

I took a couple of bites of a raspberry white chocolate scone, which was delicious, and waited for him to make sense.

"I still have some business interests," he said, "although I'm no longer in charge of any of them. One of them is a florist consortium. They have a blog and a website, usually full of the regular ads— suggestions for 'the power of flowers," seasonal ideas for beautifying your home, but lately, the website has taken a dark turn. Suddenly, they are interested in funeral arrangements, and in each one there is a reference to me."

"A reference to you?"

"Never fully stated. Always with my initials or perhaps my first name—not many Miles around that are as old as I am. Then there is a cryptic message that says something supposedly warm and loving but decidedly not."

He waved the server over. "More tea and some of those frosted cookies that look like Christmas trees."

"I see you haven't lost your sweet tooth," I said.

"Not my sweet tooth, nor any of my appetites. Eat, drink, and be merry because tomorrow—"

"You really think it's that serious?" I asked.

"Could be. I'm a nice guy, but not when it comes to business. You can't be a nice guy and come out on top. You can use your excess money for charities, and I do that. When I do crush the little guy, I usually invite him to stay on as a board member. That satisfies a few of them."

His eyes lit up when the cookies arrived. "You have to taste these, they're delicious."

I took a bite, while he crunched his way through two of them.

"Shortbread like our English cook used to make," he said. "Of course, she'd think it was blasphemy to frost them, but things can't be too sweet for me."

"Miles, as you were saying—the florist website?"

"Always in a hurry to get to the point, aren't you?" He paused to finish the last cookie and wash it down with tea. "I have to ask you, Flo, do you ever have any fun? You're a little uptight, like your father, if you don't mind my saying so."

"I do mind, but that's beside the point. You invited me here under false pretenses. You said you wanted me to play Mrs. Claus to your Santa, but what's really going on, Miles?"

"All right, I'll tell you." Miles pulled out a printed copy of a floral design newsletter, now advertising fitting tributes to loved ones who had passed away. "Here, read it yourself."

I took the printed page of several floral arrangements with suggested titles beneath them.

For the boss:

Rest in peace M.T.

You held our feet to the fire,

and look how the business thrived.

FOR THE PARTNER:

For Miles; We never fully

understood one another until now.

No more arguments or bad feelings.

FROM THE SECRETARY:

I will miss your smile if not your behavior.

RIP to the boss I would never disappoint."

I SHOOK MY HEAD. "These are peculiar, I agree, but they don't directly threaten you."

"Look at the date of death included on each one— December 24, this year."

"So you think that's when someone might try to kill you? At the party?"

"I do."

"But no one would be cruel enough to do you in at a celebration for children, surely, even if they hated you enough to kill you."

"You misunderstand. The party is not for the children, it's for the benefactors."

"Oh." I motioned to the server and asked for another scone with some lemon curd and clotted cream. I was a stress eater.

"These particular epithets seem to mean something to you," I said, pointing to the page he'd given me.

"They do. The first—keeping their feet to the fire. That's an allusion to a very unfortunate incident in my early days with a tire company I owned. Terrible fire. No one was killed but several people were badly burned, scarred for life. Of course, I settled all claims, but the unfortunates had to live with their deformities. As the person says, my business thrived."

"You have a list of the people harmed?"

"Most of them are dead by now, as I should be. There might be one or two left in a nursing home somewhere—they'd all be over eighty by now."

"Can you get me a list of their relatives who might still bear a grudge?"

"After fifty years?"

"Well, someone appears angry enough to wish you harm," I said.

"My secretary will get it to you."

"Speaking of secretaries, what does this one mean? Were some of your affairs with your secretaries?"

"A few. I need pretty things and pretty people around me, so all my secretaries have been very attractive. But if a secretary said no to my request for something more, I accepted that."

"Really?" I was becoming disgusted with Miles. How could my father have been friends with this man?

"Don't look at me like that, Flo. That's the look your father would give me. I am a man who enjoys life's pleasures. That's how I was born. That's why I never married, and if a woman said no to me, I took that at face value."

"And if she was your secretary, did you fire her for her refusal?"

Miles hesitated. "I didn't fire her. You might say I found her a more amenable place to work. I always looked out for the people in my employ—no one was left high and dry."

I couldn't seem to stop shaking my head, and my sigh was long and audible.

"I think I was a life-long project for your father," Miles said. "We had many good times together. I was the bon vivant your father might have secretly wished to be. He tried to modify my behavior, and I suppose he did—a bit. He made me look at the consequences of my actions, even if he couldn't stop me from the behavior itself."

"The partner? Who does that refer to?" I asked.

"I've had dozens of partners, so that's a hard one. I argued with all of them and bought most of them out. Only a few left angry. There was one in particular—Noella Newsome. She's the one who writes the blog you're holding. She originally had a very exclusive flower shop designed to meet each customer's fantasy. She was an artist with flowers—a maestro I'd have to say. She hated it when I turned her idea into a thriving business with a chain of shops focused on profit. Took away her magic she said."

"She's still alive?" I asked.

"Definitely. She was a very young woman when I took her under my wing. She's in her fifties now. I don't think she's the one. She recently came to visit me, saying she was ready to forgive me and asked if she might provide floral arrangements for the party."

"And you agreed?"

"Of course. She knows I'll pay her well, and I know the arrangements will be spectacular."

"And perhaps deadly. Was she one of your conquests?" I asked.

"Only briefly. When she got pregnant and I reminded her I was not the marrying kind, that was the end of things. I settled with her over the child and the business. She went her way, and I went mine. The child, a girl who is in her twenties now, is working with Noella I think. All is well."

"Good grief," I said. "Here is the most obvious suspect, and you tell me all is well. She wants to decorate for your Christmas party. Her name is Noella, for goodness sakes, and maybe, just maybe she has a wicked sense of justice—Noella comes at Christmas Eve to finish off Santa Claus."

"I must say that thought never occurred to me." Miles looked bewildered. I began to wonder if he was losing a few marbles in his old age.

"You told me the children of all your relationships were taken care of until they reached their majority."

"They were. Handsomely, I must add."

"And by majority, you mean the money stopped when they turned twenty-one?" I asked.

"Yes. I believe people should make their own fortunes, not live off mine." He smiled at me a little sheepishly. "I did put a trust in my will for each child I sired. Your father insisted on that."

"Do they know that?"

Miles shrugged. "I never told them."

"So Noella's daughter, in her twenties, has only recently lost her income from you, and she may or may not be aware that if you died, more money would come."

"I see where you're headed. I'm better off to her dead than alive. But, of course, that's true for the other children as well—if they know about the will."

"Yes, Miles, you have quite a long list of potential murderers. A staggering list I might say for a man who sees himself as straightforward and fair minded."

For the first time, I saw Miles's face cloud over. The normal twinkle in his eyes disappeared and the ready smile was missing. "You are so like your father, Flo—making me see what is right in front of my face. It appears I do have a staggering number of people who might wish me dead. Perhaps, I should simply let that happen. I'm an old man, and this would most likely be quick."

Despite his words, Miles looked frightened, more like a young child than an old man. He looked like someone who needed to be reassured.

I put my hand on his arm. He seemed so vulnerable. Maybe this was the way he made people care about him no matter what kind of scoundrel he could be.

"Look," I said. "I will be at your side during the party. You've met Kate, my assistant—you know how competent she is. You haven't met Maude, but she has become a dear friend who can talk almost anyone into telling her the truth. She's a kind of mother confessor. She'll wander the crowd—assuming we don't know before then who means to murder you."

Miles flinched at the word murder.

"Thank you, Flo." He squeezed my hand a little longer than necessary and leaned in as if he might kiss me on the lips.

"Miles, you were my father's friend. I am too old for this nonsense and we're practically family."

Miles sat up straight and placed his hand in his lap. "You see, I do take no for an answer."

I ignored that.

"What I need from you is a comprehensive list of all the people who might be eager for your death. If you have contact information, so much the better. Kate will track everyone down."

"I'll get that information for you by this evening."

"Send it to Kate." I gave him her email. "Include the name of the lawyer who drew up the will. We'll need to talk to him. Please give him your permission for us to do so."

Miles nodded. "You'll be checking up to see if I did what I told you I would do. So like your father."

He stood and held the chair for me. I assumed it was for me and not because he needed to steady himself. He called for the check and placed a generous amount of money on the table. "A Christmas bonus," he said, when the server looked at him in surprise.

I stood and watched as he put his coat on. A person mysteriously appeared at his side, handed him a cane, and took his arm.

"Flo," Miles said, "this is Jim, my personal assistant. I'll put him on my list of suspects." He turned to the tall, muscular man beside him and smiled. "Ever been on a suspect list before?"

"Not for years," Jim said with a matching grin.

"Someone wants to kill me," Miles said.

"I'm sorry to hear that, sir. I'll never get such a good job again if you croak. I'll do my best to keep you alive."

Miles laughed and patted the arm that held him upright.

"We have a lot to do." I said. "Thank you for the tea. Nice to meet you, Jim. Stay alert."

"I will, Miss Wellington."

"You know me?"

"Everyone knows you, Miss Wellington, and the success you've had preventing murders. You'll save the day, I know you will. I'll stay close by if you need any help."

"Thank you, Jim—"

"Jim Argyle, like the socks."

I left and got home in time for a drink before dinner.

WE GATHERED in the library around a robust fire. Marianne, our cook, had left us a tray of hors d'oeuvres, and Kate and I were finishing our first Scotch of the evening as I summarized my day. Maude sipped on her white wine.

"So that's it," I said. "That's everything I know. Father loved Miles, but he was always afraid Miles might seduce me. God knows he tried. Anyway, that's irrelevant."

"Irrelevant, unless I should add you to the suspect pool," Kate said, handing each of us a copy of the list Miles's secretary had compiled. "The secretary even put herself on the list. She said Miles had promised her an annuity for life if and when he died. She said she expected he might outlive her."

"There are almost one hundred names here," I said.

"Yes. I Googled the floral consortium and found the website. It seems Noella's daughter Feliz handles the monthly newsletter. She approves everything that appears there."

"Including the odd funeral wreath suggestions?" I said.

"Feliz claimed to be surprised about those when I pointed out the details. She said someone must have hacked into the system to add the initials and the date of the person's demise. She had no idea who might have done that."

"Did you believe her, Kate?" I asked.

"It was hard to tell over the phone. I think we might know more if we talk to her in person."

"I'll plan to do that tomorrow," I said.

"The list I gathered came from a number of sources," Kate said. "Mr. Tanner made a lot of enemies or perhaps frenemies is a better description—people who claimed a close friendship but would benefit from his death." Kate looked over the list. "You can delete the following people—they have either recently died or profit more from his staying alive." She gave us each a pencil. "I know how you like to be hands on, Flo, so I thought we'd do this together. If you have any question about why I'm eliminating someone from the list, let me know."

The list was assembled in alphabetical order with a description of the person involved and their relationship to Miles.

"You have been busy, Kate," I said.

"Maude helped greatly. She's almost as good at internet stalking as I am."

Maude blushed and then smiled at Kate. For a moment I felt that old unwelcome tug of jealousy. Did Maude and Kate have a relationship I could not share? My father always warned me that three was a difficult number. One person often felt left out.

"Nonsense," I said aloud.

"Nonsense?" Kate and Maude said together.

"Sorry, I was daydreaming. I'm ready."

We started with people who had died and did not have descendants that might want something from Miles. That knocked off almost forty people.

"Great," I said.

"Next, we'll go through people who benefit more from keeping Miles alive," Kate said.

That was a shorter list, but we managed to eliminate twenty names including James Argyle, Jr. Below his name was another Argyle.

"Who's this?" I asked. "James Argyle, Senior. Jim's father?"

"Yes, Jim's father. Still alive, in his sixties with a bone to pick with Miles. Miles forced him to retire as his personal assistant—said he was too old to do the physical hands-on work that might be required in the next years. His son took over."

"So what's the problem there?" I asked.

"He didn't go without a fuss. Apparently, there was also a drinking problem. He gets a lump sum of money from Miles when he dies. That's how Miles got him to go quietly into that dark night. Jim claims he's estranged from his old man."

"So," I said, "the father would benefit from Miles's death, and perhaps the son would as well. Maybe, the two are not as estranged as young Jim suggests."

"We'll leave them both on the list for now," Kate said, "and I'll try to check that out tomorrow."

Things got tedious. We ate dinner in the library on tray tables as we discussed the remaining names to see who could be safely eliminated.

"Much of this relies on Miles's memory of people he's wounded," I said, "and his secretary's honest rendition of that."

"I spoke with Miles briefly," Kate said. "He's sharp as a tack and frightened, no matter his attempts at bravado. I had Maude tackle the secretary. You know how good she is at getting people to speak the truth."

"I think the secretary can be taken off the list," Maude said. "She's been working for the old man, as she calls him, for ten years and likes him—despite his many peccadilloes. She seems to know all of them, and she also strikes me as a good judge of character."

"Excellent," I said. "Tomorrow, you can go over the list of remaining suspects with her and see what additional information she can give you."

"What will you do tomorrow?" Kate asked.

"I'll visit Noella and her daughter, Feliz. I'll see what the plans are for the party and perhaps get an idea about whether or not those two could be involved in the threat against Miles. Let's get to bed and tackle all this in the morning. I suppose I will need a costume to play Mrs. Claus."

"Already done." Kate produced a hideous outfit complete with a wig that was hanging on a hook in the hallway. "I don't think it will need a bit of altering," she said with a broad smile.

Maude had the decency to look away and turn her smile into a cough.

"Are you sick, Maude?" I asked with a broader smile.

I switched that off and grabbed the costume in its plastic bag. "Enough of this nonsense. What we all need is a good-night's sleep."

I took the outfit upstairs and tried it on in the privacy of my own bedroom. As Kate speculated, it needed no altering.

I stood tall, pushed my shoulders back, tucked in my belly, which I had to admit was beginning to protrude a bit more than I liked. I would have to talk with my personal trainer about that. Of course, she would say I should simply eat less.

It was impossible to get good help these days.

Even so, I could look dignified in this ridiculous outfit if I tried—that was a relief. And I had to do whatever was required to save a man's life, even if that person might deserve to be skewered.

I caught myself.

Miles was not the hero I'd imagined him to be, but my father had loved him. He wasn't the devil either, just a man with some insatiable appetites as he said, and a man who didn't seem to expect any consequences for his misbehavior.

I slept soundly, secretly pleased this would not be a dull Christmas.

We all got up early to attend to our various chores. Marianne fixed us a breakfast of bacon, eggs, and French toast. I thought about eating less, so I could present a more imposing figure as Mrs. Claus. That idea lasted about as long as it took Marianne to bring in her strawberry jam and fresh-baked sunrise muffins. Life was too short for such nonsense.

Kate, Maude, and I split up after breakfast and agreed to meet back for a late lunch. I contacted Noella who said she'd be happy to meet me at her boutique. She wouldn't be decorating for the party until the following morning.

All fine, I said. I found it helpful to see people more than once when deciding if they were potential murderers.

The boutique, Floral Fantasies, was charming. I arrived when it opened at ten, and it was bustling with people picking up pre-ordered Christmas arrangements. Each was unique and exquisite. I wondered if I was too late to get one for our table.

I stood to one side and watched as the girls at the cash registers rang up the sales. The prices were equally exquisite. Noella had a big crew working that day, but, even so, it seemed she must be making money hand over fist.

I caught her after the first wave of customers had left.

"I'm doing very well," she said, "thank you for asking. My customers seem to be grateful for the way I listen and create what they want. We are busy, but I can squeeze in something for you. What do you like especially?"

I had never stopped to think about what I liked in the way of flowers. If Maude were here, she'd know exactly what would suit. "I'll leave that up to you. Probably a low piece for the table. Long but low so we can talk over it and see one another."

"Of course. You dine by candlelight?" she asked.

"We do, as a matter of fact, on Christmas Eve and Christmas night."

"And the color of your dining room walls?"

"A deep green," I said.

"I'll come up with something. I'll have it ready for you tomorrow morning." She looked around. "I'm sorry I can't get it finished before then."

"No problem. I'll meet you at the venue tomorrow morning and pick it up there."

"That would be perfect." Noella smiled at me. She might have been in her fifties, but she looked younger. She had lovely thick black hair pulled back in a bun and a smile of perfectly white, perfectly straight teeth. I had no trouble identifying her daughter who had precisely the same hair and teeth and was manning one of the registers.

Noella followed my gaze. "My daughter, Feliz," she said. "Born on Christmas Eve twenty-three years ago. She's a godsend."

Noella waved her over.

"Miss Wellington, this is my daughter. Feliz, Miss

Wellington is a good friend of Miles's. She's agreed to play Mrs. Claus at the event tomorrow."

"I've heard so much about you, Miss Wellington—all your adventures. You should write a book about them."

"Thank you." Writing a book about my Old Dames Protection Agency was the last thing I intended to do. "I'll come to the venue tomorrow morning. Perhaps you can both put me to work. I like to be useful."

Did they pause just a bit?

"I won't get in the way, I promise."

Noella smiled. "It's not that at all. It's mostly heavy lifting that we'll be doing early in the morning, but if you don't mind helping us make sure the flowers on the tables look right, that would be wonderful. Say around eleven or twelve. I'll have your centerpiece ready for you by then. The gala starts at two, so perhaps you can come and stay."

"Sounds perfect. I wonder if I might talk with you, Feliz, for just a moment. You are in charge of the online newsletter?"

"Yes," Feliz said, "but I've already spoken with your assistant Kate. I have no idea how Miles's name appeared in the advertisement for the funeral flowers or how the date was marked as December 24th. It's disturbing."

Before I could ask more, Noella stepped in. "You're needed in the backroom, Feliz," she said. "I'm sorry, Ms. Wellington, it's our busiest day."

"Of course."

I left the shop before eleven, which meant I had time to check in with Miles before going home. He had a home office. I could have announced my arrival, but I thought perhaps an unannounced visit might be more informative. His butler greeted me at the door.

"Hello, Miss Wellington. Miss Merriwether just left if you were hoping to catch her here."

"No, thank you, Malcolm. I really came to speak with Miles for a few minutes if he's available."

"He'll make time for you, I'm sure. He's in his office. Please come in."

"Do you mind if I just surprise him? I know the way."

"I'm sure that will be fine." Malcolm disappeared like all good butlers of days past, and I headed upstairs. Everything about the place looked the same except for an elevator, which hadn't been there on my last visit. I imagined it allowed Miles to live pretty much as he'd always lived in that house. I'm not sure why I was so intent on the element of surprise. As far as I knew, Miles was keeping nothing from me. Why would he?

On the upstairs landing I turned left and found Jim lurking outside the door to Miles's office. He jumped when I called his name.

"Oh, Miss Wellington, you startled me. I . . . I thought I heard Miles calling for me and I was just listening at the door to see if he might need me."

I smiled and didn't bother to knock. I opened the door to see Miles at his desk, head down over some papers that he tucked away when he saw me.

"To what do I owe this visit, Flo? Not that I'm complaining."

He waved Jim away and waited until he closed the door.

"Really, why have you come here unannounced?"

"I like to see a potential victim in his natural environment. What are the papers you don't want me to see?"

Miles didn't speak immediately.

I used the time to look around the office. The desk was cluttered with files exactly the way I remembered it from long-ago visits. Miles never had one project going. It was always more like a hundred. It seemed that hadn't changed in his old age.

The paneled walls were covered with framed photographs

of him next to one important figure after another. It was a who's who of famous men and women from the last seventy years.

"I wanted to attend to some last minute arrangements," he said, "just in case something happened to me."

"You are taking this seriously," I said. "Why did you tuck them away when I came in?"

"They're private and have nothing to do with the threats against me. What are you really doing here?" he asked.

What *was* I doing here?

"Somehow, I thought it might be a good idea to simply pop in on you. See what your life looked like these days. See who might be around you. Sometimes I can pick up negative vibrations, nuances that way."

"Have you gone new-age on me?" Miles asked. "I don't mind, but I know your father would be horrified."

"No. I'm simply a person who needs all the details I can get. I need to see things for myself. It's one reason I visited Noella this morning at her boutique."

"And, what did you think?"

"Frankly, I think she's a lovely woman with an equally lovely daughter. Her business is thriving and her work is remarkable. As you said it was."

"Any negative vibes?" Miles asked.

"None. Other than the fact they were too busy to speak to me."

"Good. As I told you, she's highly successful, but as you say, you need to see everything for yourself. I'm glad she can come off the suspect list."

"I didn't say that. I'll keep Noella and Feliz on my list a little longer."

"Did you discover anything else in my household that I don't know about?"

"Why was Jim hovering outside your door?"

"Jim is intent on taking care of me. He wants to be nearby in case I need anything. Simple as that."

I nodded. "Who else is in the house?"

"My butler, of course, but you've known him for years. A couple of housemaids and the cook. The cook was recommended by your father, so I don't think she's about to poison me. I pay her well. As to the housemaids, they float in and out. I never see them."

I stood up. "I think the problem is most likely to occur at the party, not in this house. Take care, Miles, and keep Jim at your side. I'll be on your other side as Mrs. Claus."

"That will be delightful, my dear."

I reached over to shake his hand and pretended to lose my balance—putting a hand on his desk to steady myself. I managed to scatter his papers and then insisted on helping him straighten up. He grabbed for the secret papers, but I beat him to it.

I held in my hands an article from the New England Journal of Medicine on *Forms of Ataxia, New Treatment Options*.

"What's this?" I asked.

"I told you it had nothing to do with the case. I've been a little unsteady on my feet and my physician suggested I read it. I hope you won't go blathering this around to anyone."

"I don't blather, Miles." I felt deeply offended, and Miles could see that.

"I know you'll be discreet," he said. "I just hate this business of getting old, and I'd like to keep my ailments to myself."

"As you wish."

I left and arrived home to find Maude and Kate gathered around the dining room table.

"Tomorrow, we'll have a lovely centerpiece for Christmas," I told them.

I recounted my experience, omitting the article Miles tried to hide from me.\"I spoke with the lawyer," Kate said, "and no one has inquired about the will, but he didn't know who Miles might have told about his intentions. The trusts had been set up a few years ago for any offspring who could verify their relationship via DNA."

"The secretary was very helpful," Maude said, "and I think we can narrow the field a bit."

Marianne brought us lunch consisting of clam chowder and crusty bread. "Fruit and cheese for dessert if that suits you?"

"Thank you," Kate said, "that's perfect."

We settled into our usual seats and ate quietly. Father had always said no business conversations were appropriate while eating a good meal. Over coffee, Kate distributed a revised list of suspects. We were now down to twenty-nine.

"I'm not promising it's a complete list," she said, "just our best guess."

"Twenty-nine," Maude said, "that's a lot."

We reviewed them one by one and rearranged them into priority lists. Those with the most to gain by Miles's death. Those who might feel most harmed by him. Those who appeared to be the most dangerous. By that, Kate meant people who had had some previous run-in with the law.

"Interesting," I said as I looked over the list of those people with a history of violence. "Jim Argyle and his father have both been arrested for assault and battery."

"Yes," Kate said, "and Miles bailed them out each time."

"Miles is a strange mix," I said, "apparently unaware when he does harm but always ready to help a friend or an employee."

"That's precisely what his secretary thinks," Maude said. "According to her, Miles can't stand suffering and seems to be oblivious to the idea that he could be the source of anyone's pain."

I looked around for something sweet to eat beyond the

healthy fruit and cheese. Maude stood, left the room, and reappeared with a box of See's Candies. "My granddaughter sent me these from California. She's in Carmel for the holidays with a new beau. I had him checked out by every source I could find and he seems legit. I even had someone in the financial world make sure he had the money he claims to have."

"Why, Maude, I'm impressed," I said. "First, that you no longer have simple faith in the goodness of people, and secondly, that you knew I was searching for candy."

"You have hardened my heart a bit," Maude said, "but mostly in a good way. As to the candy, everyone knows about your sweet tooth. I saved the lemon chocolate truffles for you."

I grabbed both of them. "Speaking of a sweet tooth, Miles has one that makes mine look microscopic. I think that's how he's lived his life—indulging himself at every turn. If something appeals to him, he takes advantage of it."

Maude nodded. "His secretary said he doesn't mean to be malicious—he simply grabs what he wants, in business and in life."

I finished both chocolates and passed the box around. No one else partook.

"One chocolate and I'll eat the whole box," Kate said.

Maude passed it back to me. "I'm not much on sweets."

That statement to me was like saying I'm not much on air —I can take it or leave it. I thought about the Mrs. Claus outfit and decided I'd save the rest of the box for Christmas morning.

"I wonder if we can narrow our search," I said. "Perhaps, we need two sets of people.

The group of people we might call sociopaths—those with no conscience who would kill Miles for his money—and a second group. I'll call them the invisible wounded—those people who have been harmed by Miles in a way that he has not noticed or rectified."

"That would eliminate most of his love affairs and their offspring," Kate said. "He paid them well and has made provisions for them in his will."

"Which they may or may not know about," Maude said. "His secretary said he was not a boastful man in his private affairs."

"I think she's right. Even in business, he rarely boasted," I said. "That's something my father admired about him. He loved his pictures with celebrities, but he kept those in his office. He isn't a name dropper, and he doesn't say a great deal about his wealth."

"Or where it comes from," Kate said.

"Point taken," I said. "Let's divide up the lists and see where we get. Maude, perhaps you can look for the wounded who have gone unnoticed—you're good at that. You could hang out in his home this afternoon and see what you can find —start with the secretary again. It might mean we discover more names.

"Kate, you can track down the sociopaths, those people who simply want to take advantage of Miles. See if there are any women in the list of relationships that might have been taking Miles for a ride, not the other way around. I'll do a little quiet thinking in my room."

"Nap time?" Kate asked.

"I do my best thinking when I'm asleep," I said. "We'll meet for dinner."

I went upstairs and climbed under my comforter. I studied the list and thought about Miles before I fell asleep. Why had my father loved him so? Every story he told me about Miles, he told with joy and laughter.

My father was a person who always did the right thing. When my mother died, I was two, and Father took on the responsibility of raising me. He didn't shift it off to nannies, although I certainly had nannies. He was much more hands on, and while I don't think he saw me as a burden, I'm quite sure I cramped his style.

Nothing slowed Miles down, and I think my father must have been envious. Perhaps he lived a vicarious life through him. Father never remarried, saying no one could compete with my mother's love for me or for him.

For a moment, I felt sad.

Then I turned my attention back to Miles. Who was it he'd hurt without realizing it? Who was it he couldn't pay off with the right amount of money? It seemed to me it had to be about love. Unrequited love or someone who felt abandoned when he moved on.

That's as far as I got before I fell asleep. Too soundly and for too long. I woke up in time for happy hour, but I didn't feel happy. I felt groggy, annoyed with myself and the world. Snippets of dreams surfaced— a missed plane, a sense I had too much to do and no time to do it. I was supposed to pick up all the pieces left by a careless person. That had to be Miles. I wondered who else felt like they were picking up all the pieces?

Hmm. His secretary for one. But Maude had found her a pleasant individual, not someone who appeared to be harboring deep resentments.

Kate, Maude and I met for dinner— a pre-Christmas Eve dinner, which was always a surprise. Marianne had outdone herself. Each year she chose a holiday meal from a different nationality.

This year it was Kūčios from Lithuania—twelve cold dishes, no dairy or meat. Marianne explained it to us as we ate. It was normally served on Christmas Eve. She said it was a mixture of pagan and Christian traditions depending on who you talked to. We sampled everything from eel to herring to sauerkraut and ended with spanguolių kisielius (cranberry kissel). One had to taste each dish in order to live to see the next holiday season. That got my attention, and I complied.

We toasted Marianne with some very fine champagne and then retired to the library where we went over what if anything we'd discovered. A few people came off the list. One or two were added, but we weren't any closer to identifying a would-be murderer.

"It will be all hands on deck tomorrow," I said. "I'm still looking for the person Miles unwittingly wounded."

CHRISTMAS EVE DAY dawned cold and bright. Snow was expected by evening. Fortunate timing for Santa's sleigh, Maude said.

I dressed carefully. Kate had created a hidden pocket for me in the costume. I put my antique revolver, a gift from my father, into it. Kate had taken me out to a firing range to make sure I could use it without blowing off my own hand. I could. She agreed to dress as an elf with her own firearm—most likely more than one.

Maude dressed as a guest.

Miles had made it clear no police would be present at the party. They could get trigger happy and spoil the whole event, he said. Besides, everyone could spot a policeman from a mile away and that would destroy the carefree spirit he was hoping for.

Once Miles made up his mind, there was no changing it. It would be up to us to save the day, and we'd do our best.

Two hundred guests had RSVP'd. When Miles threw a party, it was always unforgettable.

I went over to the venue as promised at eleven. Noella was busy directing where the giant shipment of flowers should go. There were stations for the table arrangements, the grand bouquets for the head table, the pots of decorated Christmas trees throughout the hall.

I waited until she spotted me. She ran over with a lovely table decoration—mine as it turned out. Indescribable and gorgeous. Dark greens, light greens, white roses. No glitzy gold or red ribbons. Somehow she knew I wouldn't like that.

"It's perfect, just perfect," I said.

"I'm so pleased," Noella said. "We'll leave it on the side table where people pick up their name tags if you don't mind. Then you can take it home when you leave. Feliz put it together."

I saw Feliz working on the table arrangements and walked over to thank her. I also offered to help.

"You can help me most by sitting right there and checking each table arrangement as I finish them. We have twenty tables. Anything that doesn't look quite right, just let me know. It's wonderful to have a second eye."

"Why is everyone in costume?" I asked Feliz. "It must be hard to work in those."

"It's simply that some people may come early, so we wanted everyone to look festive." I sat at the table and watched the people passing in and out of the room. If the person in question wanted to harm or kill Miles, wouldn't they try to do it in a way that couldn't be traced to them? If they were angry enough, I suppose they could just fire at close range. But why then, do all the preamble? The threats were subtle, and I suspected the attempt at murder might be subtle as well.

I signed off on each arrangement as it was passed to me. Nothing needed changing. I had about five minutes between arrangements and it didn't matter much if a couple got stacked up on the table. As I passed each one along, a helper in costume as an elf or a reindeer took the arrangement and placed it on one of the tables. I watched to make sure no one tampered with the flowers.

I'd read enough Agatha Christie to know how deadly some plants could be and how much Agatha loved to poison people.

Still, it was unlikely the table arrangements would be tainted. More likely, someone might tamper with the arrangement on the head table close to Miles. That was the one to watch. I stood, stretched, and walked around the room. I'd told Maude and Kate to arrive around twelve. They came early, and I greeted them at the door.

"Kate, will you hang out in the kitchen? See what you can find out about the caterers and the food. See if any special dish is being prepared for Miles or the head table. Maude, will you mingle? You can pretend to wish to be helpful, but don't get caught up in any particular project that might distract you. You have a good eye for what people might be feeling. That's what I want to know about—anyone who seems anxious or angry."

"Got it," they both said.

I continued to wander around the space. At least two dozen people were hard at work decorating windows and walls with garlands. Silver and gold balls were being hung from the ceiling. Above them a net of snowflake-stenciled white balloons was tacked up to be released at the end of the event I assumed.

That caught my eye. What if one of the balloons held something more than hot air—like a deadly gas or a heavy object. Perhaps, I was letting my imagination run away with me. How would our murderer make sure other people weren't harmed? Of course, if he were one of the suspects that had no conscience like a sociopath, he might not care who else got hurt.

So many people I didn't know or recognize. So many people that weren't on any of our lists. Worse than that many of them were in costume. Elves, sugar plum fairies, reindeer—all with masks.

I sat back down at the table and signed off on three more arrangements. They were all lovely. They had a common color scheme but each was original. They were going to be auctioned off to the highest bidder. Aim High stood to make a lot of money at this event, even though it was supposedly a celebration to say thank you to those who had already given.

I noted that the same three elves took the arrangements from my table. Actually, two elves and one reindeer. The reindeer limped slightly and seemed smaller than the rest. He was as agile as the other two but he seemed slightly twisted, perhaps from scoliosis.

I engaged him in conversation, and he took off his mask to speak to me, his headgear as well. A long cascade of golden blond hair fell around a face that was decidedly not male. She was in fact a lovely young woman.

"I'm so pleased to meet you, Miss Wellington."

Her speech was a little jerky, difficult to understand. I leaned in to hear her more clearly.

"My great grand uncle has told me so much about you," she said.

"Really, and you are?"

"Wendolyn. Wendy."

"Somehow I didn't know Miles had a sibling."

"An older brother died when Miles was quite young of Friedreich's Ataxia. He left behind a wife and daughter. The daughter was my mother. That's the reason Uncle Miles left California—he couldn't bear the memories of his brother's suffering."

"Friedreich's Ataxia? I don't know anything about that disorder," I said.

"It's a genetic affliction that runs through our family. My mother didn't have it, but she passed it on to me. Sometimes a clubfoot is an early symptom of that disorder—unfortunately that happened to me. Uncle Miles made sure I had a number of surgeries to correct that along with all the latest treatments."

She showed me the special boot she wore. "The surgeries weren't entirely successful. Uncle Miles paid for everything."

"Kind of him," I said.

Wendolyn hesitated. "Kind of him?" She picked up an arrangement. "Uncle Miles loves pretty things, pretty people. He can't tolerate ugliness. I've said too much already. Mother says I am always too open about our family secrets."

"But why should your disorder be a secret?" I asked.

"You'll need to ask Uncle Miles. It's certainly not a secret to me." She hobbled off with the arrangement. I now saw that her limp was accompanied by an unsteadiness of gait.

It was one pm when the flowers for the tables were finished. The room looked gorgeous. Miles entered a few minutes later and beckoned me to his side. We admired each others' outfits. He did look splendid as Santa. It was hard to believe the beard was fake, and the twinkle in his eye was genuine.

"You look grand, Flo."

"Might as well call me Mrs. Claus for the full effect." I towered over him, but that didn't bother either one of us. "Shall we sit before the guests arrive?"

He nodded. Jim appeared at his side and helped him to the head table. It was the first time I noticed his unsteady gait. Before, I'd chocked it up to old age.

"Miles, I met a great grandniece of yours, Wendy."

"Wendolyn is here?"

"Yes."

"I suppose that's all right. I didn't notice her, and with Wendolyn, you usually know when she's around."

"You mean she's a talker?" I asked.

"That, and other things."

"Like what, Miles?" I asked.

"Oh, things she can't help. You've seen how she walks?"

"You mean her gait?"

"Yes, and her twisted body. It's upsetting to watch her try to move around. I wish she'd just sit, stay out of sight, really."

"You can't mean that, Miles. She's your niece."

"Precisely. She's my great grandniece, and she reminds me and everyone else what's wrong with this family."

"Friedreich's Ataxia," I said.

"She *has* talked to you. That's one reason I asked her not to come. That girl simply cannot keep her mouth shut."

"She told me about her clubfoot as well."

"I'm not surprised. There's nothing unseemly about this family that she can resist talking about."

"Why does that upset you so?"

"I've done everything I can to improve her life. Friedreich's Ataxia is a terrible disease. It's based on a recessive gene which means both people have to be carriers to cause problems. God knows I've done everything in my power to stamp it out of our family.

"I made sure every woman I dated had a DNA test when those became available. I debated having a vasectomy, but I hate surgery or anything that causes pain. Others in the family had none of my scruples about passing that illness along. I tried to warn my sister she might be a carrier, but she ignored me. Wendolyn is the product of that carelessness."

I was stunned. For a minute I couldn't speak.

"Miles, she's your flesh and blood. You sound so cold when you speak about her."

"I've tried to fix her, but the disease has no cure. It was irresponsible of her mother to have her. We have enough suffering and deformity in this world without adding to it."

"She's a lovely woman," I said.

For a moment, I thought Miles might cry. "Yes," he said. "That makes it all the more unbearable. Realizing she could die at any moment of heart disease . . . like my brother."

"How old was he?"

"Twenty-three. I was twenty-two. We were like twins really, only he was sick and I seemed to be well. He died in front of me. I couldn't do a thing. I suppose it's one reason I've led the life I have. Do what you want and surround yourself with beauty. It's an ugly disease, Flo."

"You have it now, don't you?"

"I have a late onset variety, perhaps a mild case. My brother was at the other end of the spectrum, early onset, severe disease, and early death. With all the available treatments, Wendolyn may live longer than most, but to what point? I've tried to fix everything I could about her, but it wasn't enough. It will never be enough. She remains twisted and suffering, and often I can't bear to see her."

"Wendy doesn't strike me as a girl who is unhappy with her life. Have you ever talked to her about that?"

"Of course not. It's hard to sit in the same room with her. I see how she suffers, and I see what's ahead of her."

"She reminds you of your brother, or yourself perhaps?"

"Stop the Freudian analysis. That was passé fifty years ago. I turn away from ugliness and pain. End of story."

"Oh, Miles," I said, "what a desperate and narrow life you've led."

Miles looked at me as if I had slapped him in the face. He didn't speak.

I watched as Wendolyn and Feliz put the finishing touches on the centerpiece. It was heavy and they carried it together to place in front of Miles. It was perfection, at first glance.

I leaned my head in slowly to smell the flowers. If there was something deadly about them, I was quite sure Wendy would stop me. She didn't. In fact, she winked at me as if she knew what I was thinking.

As I sniffed each flower I watched as she added a little more to the arrangement. No poisonous spiders. Everything ceramic but remarkably ugly. A gnarled hand, a tiny rat, a dozen objects. I looked over at Miles who was following her hand and gazing at each object she placed below the flowers.

She took off her mask when she was done. He stared back

at her.

"I knew it was you from the way you walked," he said.

"I was sure you would recognize me—the littlest reindeer, the one you could never allow to sit at your Christmas table, too ugly for you to bear."

"I did everything I could to help you—make you beautiful and fix what I could about this family curse," Miles said.

"No. You did everything you could to make me tolerable to you. It wasn't a curse to me, Miles. I have learned to live with it. There are so many treatments now, I may outlive you."

She placed a hand over his. "All I wanted was your love. You never asked me if I wanted all the surgeries. Not once. You never seemed to care how painful they were. And when it was all done, you still couldn't bear to see me."

Miles said nothing.

I turned to Wendy.

"Are you responsible for the veiled threats against his life?"

"We all are. Noella, Feliz, even Jim and his father. Uncle Miles has hurt all of us, and we wanted him to know that. Uncle Miles was oblivious to the pain he caused others. He thought money could rectify everything."

Miles watched her as she spoke, but he said nothing.

"We wanted him to worry. To be afraid he might die. He's always been afraid of dying, even in his old age. We were glad when we heard he'd taken it seriously and that he'd enlisted you to protect him."

Wendy looked at me with what at first appeared to be a triumphant smile. It turned quickly into sadness.

"I spearheaded it. I wanted him to suffer as I had suffered —not from the disease but from the isolation. All I ever wanted was for Uncle Miles to notice me, to love me a little."

Miles hadn't moved a muscle. When Wendy finished, he looked down at the arrangement in front of him.

I let him be.

As the first guests arrived, Jim and I helped him stand at the door and greet people. The beard did a great deal to hide his stony expression. I became gracious and outgoing, something that I'm sure stunned Kate and Maude if they were watching. A few people asked if Miles was feeling all right, and I assured them he was.

The party was a huge success. The Boston Globe took dozens of pictures, sadly identifying me as the Mrs. Claus at Miles's side.

I was exhausted when we finally got home. We had our usual Christmas Eve dinner of French onion soup, sourdough bread, and a luscious pear salad.

I think we all felt sad. I know I did.

"Look how miserably Miles has lived—trying to keep his pain at bay," I said. "And poor Wendolyn."

"I think you have that part wrong," Maude said. "I got a chance to talk with her before everyone left the party. She was sorry about frightening Miles, but she wasn't unhappy about her life. Not at all. Did you know she's in medical school? Third year. She plans to get an MD PhD and study rare genetic disorders."

"Will she have time for that?" I asked. "Will she live long enough?"

"She thinks so. She assured me there are many new treatments on the horizon. With luck, she'll find more. Perhaps a genetic one. She assured me it's how she wants to spend her life."

"That is a lovely story," I said. "Has she told all that to Miles?"

"He's never asked," Maude said.

I spent a lazy week between Christmas and New Year's. That gave me time to think. So many feelings had been stirred up in me—about my father, Miles, Wendy.

I wondered if my father and I had had a heart-to-heart talk

about my mother's death—if perhaps my father could have led a happier life. But he was a Boston Brahmin born and bred, stiff upper lip, noblesse oblige. Perhaps he was content with the life he'd been given. He liked responsibility.

And what about Miles? I wondered what he was thinking and feeling.

I got a call from him on New Year's Eve day.

"Are you and Maude and Kate busy tonight?" he asked. "I'd like you to come over for a very small party."

Kate, of course, had plans for later in the evening, but she was willing to join us for an early soiree. Wendy was there along with Noella and Feliz. Jim stood in the background, the place he always stood, ready to help as needed.

Miles greeted us warmly. He looked more frail than the last time I'd seen him, and his smile had lost its shiny edges.

"Are you all right?" I asked.

"I am," he said. "This will be a hard year for me, and I doubt that I will live to see another one. I don't mind that—it's just that I have so much to learn about life. I'm wondering if I will have time to learn it all."

"Join the club, Miles," I said. "We all have so much to learn. Some of us don't seem to know that, which is the real harm. You are 'woke' now." I looked over at Kate. "Right term?"

She grimaced at me and then nodded.

Wendy stood by Miles's side and helped him sit down. She sat beside him.

"I'm not expecting miracles," she whispered to me as I sat on the other side of her, "but I'm glad to be in his presence. I'm glad to answer his questions about my life."

"I'm glad to hear he's asking them," I said.

"It seems he's more hopeful since we talked about my life. He suspects I'm smart enough to find a cure for this disease. And, in any case, he admires my grit."

"He should," I said.

"It isn't all work you know. I have a lab assistant, a class-mate, who seems to find me attractive. We have fun in and out of the lab."

That made me smile.

It was a pleasant evening, and we kept it short. None of us was getting any younger. Kate dropped us at home and headed out for parties more her own style. I never asked about them, and she never told me.

I suppose the best part of our whole story is that we had a similar gathering a year later. We'd all survived. This time, Wendolyn brought her fiancé, a delightful young man. He'd received his MD PhD the previous spring and Wendy would receive hers in June. They had lab space at Johns Hopkins and a grant to study Friedreich's Ataxia.

"They are planning a small wedding in March," Miles said, "and I hope to be there."

"You are all invited," Wendy said to me. "It will be in the south of France—that's where Pierre is from."

Her fiancé, Pierre, strode across the room, took my hand and touched it to his lips. "We would be so pleased if you could come."

I smiled and gave Kate a frantic look. "The Queen Elizabeth is no longer in service," I whispered.

"Might be time to fly," she whispered back with a malicious grin.

Miles was now confined to a wheelchair, but he seemed content and in good spirits. "It's not a bad life," he said to me, "when you don't have to pretend to be God and try to control things that you can't possibly control. Wendolyn is happy and thriving. She's lovely, isn't she?"

"Yes, Miles, she is."

THE END

5

OLD FRIENDS AND OLDER CRIMES

Maude picked up a tiny crystal ornament that had fallen from a glass Christmas tree nestled on the corner of my partners desk. "It didn't break," she exclaimed. "What luck. I guess the leather softened its fall. " She hung it back on the tree and smiled at me as if she'd just saved the baby Jesus from harm.

One thing Maude and I shared was a love of Christmas. I liked decorations to be a little understated but Maude would have none of that. She was over the top with her enthusiasm. Kate joined her in that. My brownstone was ablaze with a giant Christmas tree in the downstairs bay window. Greenery flowed up the bannister of the staircase and every fireplace mantle was decorated with angels and Santas.

I pretended to be aghast at the decorations, but I was the one who made sure every one of them was carefully wrapped and put away at the first of the year to be brought out again in early December.

Maude sat across from me at the desk once she was certain

our little tree was properly adorned. She sighed contentedly as I reviewed our financial records. Maude was almost always content, now that I'd helped her turn her life around. I, on the other hand, rarely felt satisfied.

"Look at these numbers," I said. "For all our hard work, we seem to have so little to show for it. It's not the American way."

"We have saved three lives over the past three years," Maude said. "Perhaps more, and one of them was mine. That is no trivial accomplishment and one can hardly put a price tag on a person's life. I would say we have been highly successful."

"I'd have to agree." This came from Kate, the youngest member of ODPA. "Your Old Dames Protection Agency is close to breaking even this year!"

She brought in a pot of coffee and set it on the desk with a mat beneath. Beside it was a decanter of the best brandy money could buy. I had to admit I had trained Kate well during our many years of partnership.

"By my count," I said, "we've been in business three years and been paid a total of a few thousand dollars. We are still not making a profit."

"It really depends on how you look at it, Flo," Kate said. "We've done dozens of small jobs, telling people to back off when it appeared they were bullying or threatening someone. Occasionally, I've had to travel to make that point in person. We've gotten paid for those requests. See this line in your accounting book?"

I looked where she pointed. I had kept a list called "Trivial Pursuits and Expenses."

"Look at the totals," Kate said. "I wish you'd let me put this on Quicken. It would make all our lives so much easier."

"I like this method, thank you very much. It's all here in black and white, can't be hacked, et cetera, et cetera."

"Fine, Flo," Kate said. "Look at the totals—in black and white."

I did.

"Hmm. It seems we spent a little over five hundred dollars this last year and made close to five thousand," I said. "But these were such unimportant efforts, threats that amounted to nothing."

"Perhaps to you," Kate said, "but these people were very grateful, and I made sure they paid their fees."

"By strong-arming them?" I asked. Kate was the brawn behind my brain. She was young and fit and knew how to use a gun. She had her own armory, locked away in my basement, and she had several other useful approaches to subduing people through a smattering of martial arts.

"No, I didn't strong arm them. They were grateful for my help, and unlike you, I made them sign a contract. Anyway, the point is that we are very close to breaking even. In another year or so, we might just see a profit."

I smiled. "That would be very nice. We'd no longer be a hobby to the IRS, more like a thriving enterprise."

"It's not as if you need the money," Kate said, "or the tax breaks."

"True, but I do want to be more than a charitable foundation for potential victims of high crimes and misdemeanors."

"We're getting far more requests than we can handle as a matter of fact," Kate said. She thumbed through a stack of mail. "Here's one from someone who says she knows you."

She handed me an envelope, postmarked Atlanta. Who did I know in Atlanta? I stared at it.

"Read it," Maude said. "I can't stand the suspense."

I skimmed the letter. "Yes," I said when I finished. "It's from an old friend of mine. Actually, she's not so old. Younger than you are, Kate. We met when she was here several years ago for a conference on childhood obesity. I went because I so liked the idea of healthy school lunches. She's a lovely woman with a funny name. She insisted I call her Ditie—seems her father named her Aphrodite and her mother wouldn't stand for it—so she became Mabel Aphrodite Brown. She's a pediatrician in Atlanta."

"A pediatrician needs our help?" Maude asked. "Or is this just an early Christmas letter to let you know how she's doing?"

"No, no, it's a request for help. Do we have any plans for Christmas this year?"

Kate shook her head. "You said you wanted to leave the calendar open to see what might pop up."

"Are we traveling again?" Maude asked with obvious delight. "I don't think I've been to Atlanta except when I was passing through to catch a plane somewhere else."

"Perhaps we should go," I said. "Dr. Brown says she needs our expertise. She said she'd sent me a few emails, but as she got no response, she decided to write a letter."

"Smart girl," Kate said. "Most people don't realize you never look at your emails, so they think you're snubbing them. This woman sounds persistent."

"Very persistent," I said. "And quite the detective. She's been written up in the Atlanta papers."

"*That* Dr. Brown!" Kate said. "Yes, I've heard about her. There was a very sad story about the death of a close friend of hers that left two orphaned children. She had to protect them from criminals."

"Yes, and she did," I said. "She's a woman after my own heart."

"If she's a detective in her own right, why does she need us?" Maude asked.

"She has her work and her children," I said. "More than that it seems the potential danger is in an assisted living facility. Two people have died under mysterious circumstances and a third is frightened she might be next."

"My goodness," Maude said, "we *are* needed."

"Yes. Obviously, Ditie can't do a great deal without looking very out of place, but you and I, Maude, could fit right in."

Maude grinned. "How soon do we leave?"

Kate, often the voice of reason, asked how Ditie knew there was a problem. Was this a relative of hers?

"No. She says it's a relative of someone who works in the refugee clinic with her." I reread the letter. "Actually, it's the grandmother of one of the nurses at the clinic."

"And the police are not involved for some reason?" Kate asked.

"Ditie says the police did investigate the two deaths but found no evidence to confirm a case of murder. It seems the resident who is so upset is not the most reliable witness. She has Parkinson's and has started hallucinating. It's very hard to know where the truth lies. That's why Ditie wants us there."

"Intriguing," Kate said. "I guess our Christmas schedule is no longer open. I suppose we're driving?"

"Of course. The sooner we get there, the better. Can you drive us straight through?"

Kate sighed. "It's twenty hours at least. If you let me take a nap when I need to I suppose I can."

"Excellent. Ditie says we can stay with her, but I think we'll need to find a way to stay at the facility."

"I'll look into it," Kate said. "You'll have to be my grand-mother, and you, Maude, may have to be her partner, if you know what I mean."

Again Maude smiled. "Whatever."

"How soon are you hoping to leave, Flo?" Kate asked.

"I was thinking sometime tomorrow."

"Tomorrow?" Kate said and sighed. "Very well. I'm going to bed. I'll check on the facility in the morning, and we'll leave after lunch. Is that soon enough?'

"I was hoping for an early start tomorrow morning," I said,

"but that will have to do. I'll call Ditie and let her know we'll be arriving sometime the following day."

The drive down was a blur. Even in a car as comfortable as ours, there wasn't quite enough room to stretch out properly. I took the front seat and reclined it as far as it would go. Maude lay in the back, curled up under a comforter.

We stopped at fast food restaurants every few hours so Kate could stretch her legs and we ate whatever passed for food in those establishments. The drive through the night was disorienting—passing big trucks, lights flashing in our windows from every angle, stopping at truck stops for gas.

I did my best to sleep through most of it, but all of us were cranky when we arrived at Ditie's house in Virginia-Highland. This was a neighborhood in Atlanta named for the streets that intersected it—Virginia and Highland—not especially imaginative, but the houses were charming. Most were bungalows like Ditie's, brick, built in the 1920s I'd guess.

We arrived on a Wednesday, which happened to be Ditie's half day at the clinic. That meant she was home to greet us, along with her friend Lurleen du Trois. Really, Lurleen du Trois. I'd met Ditie before but never her friend. Ditie hadn't changed since the last time we'd met. She was short and round with hair that frizzled all over her head, and she had the warmest smile you could imagine. It was impossible not to smile back at her.

"You haven't aged a bit," she said to me. She hugged me and didn't seem to mind my stiff response. "I always forget New Englanders are not big huggers," she said. "In the South, it's the first thing you do whether you actually know the person or not."

She brought us into the house while Lurleen grabbed some of our luggage and kissed each of us on both cheeks. She also had a translucent smile and looked ravishing in a simple pale green sheath, her auburn hair swirling around her as she knelt to pick up our luggage.

"Ditie has told me all about you and your ODPA organization," she said. "I feel as if we've known each other for years." She spoke in a kind of Southern French drawl, something I'd never heard before.

She looked to be a couple of years older than Ditie and perhaps the same number of years younger than Kate. Kate took an instant shine to her as did Maude. I'm the most reserved member of the group, so I was curious to see what the relationship was between these two women—friends or something more.

Lurleen caught my eye and explained before I had a chance to ask any direct questions. "I don't live here," she said. "I live five minutes away and help Ditie with the children when she's at work."

"Lurleen and her boyfriend, Danny Devalle, are the closest people I have to family here," Ditie explained. "Not to short-change my boyfriend—Mason Garrett. He's a detective with the Atlanta police and stays busy. I've told him you were coming, so you'll meet him at dinner."

I noticed the small emerald ring on the third finger of her left hand.

"Your boyfriend, Ditie?" Lurleen said. "Her fiancé would be a more appropriate term. They're getting married sometime this year."

"Congratulations," I said.

"Thanks. You all look exhausted." Ditie said. "I've got some soup and home-made bread if you're hungry, and then I think you should take a nap before dinner."

It was a simple, delicious lunch of cauliflower and rose-mary soup, better than most restaurants served and sour-dough bread that was spectacular. I don't gush, but Kate and Maude said it for me.

Maude and I settled into the two downstairs bedrooms while Kate slept upstairs. Ditie woke us gently at six. "Dinner at seven," she said. "Clean towels are in the bathrooms if you want to freshen up."

We gathered in the living room to discover a cluster of quiet creatures, two young children—a boy and a girl, two men, one thirty something and the other considerably older, along with a large dog and cat, both yellow. The dog ambled over to greet us, but the cat leapt down from Lurleen's lap and disappeared when we entered the room.

""You have quite the menagerie here," I said. "How in the world did we manage to hear nothing at all?" I asked.

"Hearing aides out?" Kate asked.

"Unnecessary and untrue."

"It's a small house," Ditie said, "but it has solid doors. The kids were in the family room, doing homework, and Mason and Danny just arrived."

Mason Garrett was a sturdy man in his late forties I would guess, although I was no longer a judge of age. He had a bald head, like so many people these days, but he wore it well. It set off his highly-intelligent gray eyes that softened when he smiled. Danny Devalle was another matter all together. He could be in an ad selling sports equipment. I'd buy. He was all muscle, blond hair and had outrageous good looks. It wasn't hard to match up these two with their appropriate partners.

We sat in the living room making small talk as the men served us drinks and hors d'oeuvres.

"Danny's a great cook," Ditie said. "He's responsible for the hors d'oeuvres."

"I'm not sure we'll need dinner," Kate said. "These meatballs with the yogurt dip are fantastic and I love the fig and walnut creation!"

"It's called fig and walnut *'amuse bouche'*—isn't that perfect?" Lurleen beamed.

"It certainly amuses *my* mouth," Kate said.

Dinner was simple and tasty—prime rib with roasted potatoes and asparagus. We waited to discuss what was really on everyone's mind until Ditie got the children to bed on a sleeper sofa in the family room.

"We've put the children out of their bedrooms," Maude said.

"No worries," Ditie told her. "This is a treat for them. I told them they could watch TV, and they're on Christmas vacation starting tomorrow. The TV will drown out our discussion, although if I know Lucie she'll be on top of whatever we have to say. She's already questioned me about why you're coming, and she Googled you to find out about your business—Old Dames Protection Agency—if I have that right."

"You do," I said.

She closed the French doors that separated the family room from the living room and settled on the sofa beside Mason. We kept our voices down.

Ditie began the conversation. "As I wrote in my letter to you, I work with a wonderful nurse who is very concerned about the welfare of her grandmother. Her grandmother, Alma, has been living in an assisted-living home for over a year in Decatur."

"Decatur?" Kate asked.

"A small town bordering on Atlanta," Ditie said. "Not really such a small town anymore."

"It's out of my jurisdiction," Mason Garrett said, "which is why I couldn't be part of the investigation."

"But Danny could," Lurleen said, squeezing the very muscular arm of the man seated beside her. "He's a private investigator, so he goes where he's needed."

Danny nodded. "The Decatur police were involved initially. Alma filed a complaint. It seemed two of the residents had died from a fall down the back stairs. Most of the residents are instructed to use the elevators, but these two apparently used the stairs for exercise or perhaps something else."

"Something else?" Kate asked.

"You know how old folks can get lonely and frisky," Lurleen said, and Danny blushed.

"On the stairs?" I asked. I couldn't really keep the disbelief out of my voice.

"Not on the stairs," Danny said. "There's a lounge on the third floor near the stairs with several couches, rarely used by anyone as far as I could tell. I don't know why it's there, but it's a convenient meeting place. Using the stairs would keep such encounters private."

"I assume the two individuals who died were male and female?" I said.

"They were," Danny said. "But they didn't die on the same day. They died a couple of weeks apart."

"Were they a couple?" Maude asked.

"It seems so," Danny said. "One a widow and the other with a spouse in the Alzheimer's unit next door."

"So we have lovers who died separately but in precisely the same way." I said. "The police thought they were both accidents?"

"They couldn't prove otherwise," Danny said. "The stairs are narrow and steep. Concrete. It wouldn't be hard to lose your balance and tumble down a flight. Since the second death the stairs have been closed off."

"The timing of the two deaths is curious," I said.

"Yes," Danny agreed.

"Could the second death have been a dramatic suicide, a lover who couldn't bear to live without the person who died?"

"It's possible," Ditie said. "According to Alma, Berthold was distraught after Loretta died."

"Berthold?" I asked.

"Berthold Schmidt. German," Ditie said. "Came here as a

boy before World War II. Lucky to get out when he did. His parents didn't make it."

Ditie left to check on the children and turn off the TV. "Why don't we settle around the dining room table for dessert —that way Lucie won't be able to hear what we say if she's only pretending to be asleep."

"Pretending to be asleep?" Maude asked.

"Lucie is a budding detective," Lurleen said. "Nothing gets past her. She's already helped Ditie solve one case."

Ditie nodded. "She has. When I couldn't see the forest for the trees, Lucie saw it all clearly."

We gathered once more at the table, and Ditie served us chocolate pudding cake with homemade vanilla ice cream.

"Ditie won a prize for this cake," Lurleen said proudly, "at Savannah Evan's cooking contest."

Ditie started to protest. "No prize," she said, but before she could say more, Kate jumped in.

"I love her shows! Everything is healthy and fresh." Kate paused. "I read about what happened on Savannah's estate in the *Charleston Times.* You were the celebrity detective who solved the crime, Dr. Brown."

Ditie blushed.

What was it with these people—turning red at the slightest provocation. The pudding cake was exquisite, and I commented on that. Then I asked if we might get down to business.

Kate gave me a look. "I suppose you remember Flo from your previous encounter at the conference, Ditie. She gets impatient when things don't move right along."

Ditie smiled. "I have no problem with that. It's getting late, and we *should* get on with it."

I couldn't refrain from giving Kate a triumphant smile. "So where does Alma fit into all this?"

"She's the linchpin," Ditie said. "She didn't see either of

these people fall, but she claims to have seen someone lurking in the area of the lounge and back stairs. The problem is that she sometimes sees things that aren't there. Parkinson's and hallucinations."

"You've spoken with her yourself?" I asked.

"I have," Ditie said, "but Danny has been in more direct contact. He's working as an aide there."

"I came on as soon as Alma got worried about her own safety. The facility is very short-handed, so they hired me on a temporary basis after a quick background check. The administration thought it might be an asset to have a former cop on its staff—I was with the Atlanta police force for a few years."

"That's interesting," I said. "If the administration had anything to do with these deaths, I doubt that they'd want a cop nosing around."

"That's what I thought as well," Ditie said as she began to gather the empty dishes from the table.

"I've got it, " her boyfriend, Mason, said. "You stay put and finish this conversation."

Kate offered to help, but he motioned her to sit as well.

Maude leaned over to Ditie and whispered, "You've got a good one there."

"Believe me, I know," she said.

She turned to me. "We're of the same mindset. I don't believe the administration knows any more about these deaths than we do. Of course, they want to avoid publicity. That may be one reason they were so eager to hire Danny. They don't want a murderer running loose in their facility obviously, and if Danny can quietly clear things up, all the better."

"When I called to see if they had any rooms available, they were very enthusiastic," Kate said. "Did you let them know I might try to arrange that, Ditie?"

"No."

"Isn't there a long waiting list?" Kate asked.

"I don't think so," Ditie said. "A newer facility has opened down the road with more amenities. I think these folks are desperate for new occupants."

Maude looked over at Kate. "How soon can we move in?"

"You have an appointment with the intake coordinator tomorrow at nine. The woman I spoke to said two rooms were available immediately, but I told her one would do."

"You said what?" I asked. "I'm used to my privacy."

"I want you two in the same place," Kate said. "If there is a killer running around, I don't want either of you alone—you must stick together!"

Sometimes, I felt that Kate forgot who was the CEO of this organization. "They don't have rooms with an adjoining door?"

"No, they do not."

"I suppose we can manage that for a few days," I said.

"Hopefully, it will be a matter of days and not weeks," Danny said.

"Done by Christmas," I said. "That's my deadline."

"We'll plan on having you spend Christmas here with us," Ditie said. "The children will love it."

KATE WENT with us to meet with the intake coordinator at nine. Kate presented us as sweet, slightly doddering old women who needed a gentle watchful eye from time to time. She also described us as women who liked our privacy, so no barging in on us unannounced.

The coordinator was all smiles. "We never barge in anywhere," she said. "We like our residents to be as independent as possible. Should the time ever arise where more is needed," she paused and nodded her head slightly to the right, "we have a facility for that as well."

I'd heard enough. "We're not losing our minds, I can assure you, young woman. It's simply our agility that requires a little extra care."

"No offense meant, Ms. Wells," she said.

Kate thought it better to keep our real names off the record—someone might get wind of our true occupations.

It seemed there was a choice of rooms available. We wandered through several on the first floor near the front of the establishment.

"Any toward the back of the building?" Kate asked. "Perhaps on an upper level? My grandmother hates noise."

The coordinator sighed. "We do have a few at the back of the building, but they are generally reserved for relatives who are from out of state and wish to visit for a few days. We are not allowed to use them for our long-term guests."

I snorted at that. Long-term guests indeed. The ones that never left.

Kate glared at me. "My grandmother has a cold. Nothing serious but another reason to tuck her away from your "guests" who might be vulnerable to bugs."

The woman hesitated only momentarily. "I suppose we can let you stay there on a temporary basis. They are quite beautiful rooms, part of the old estate. Not retrofitted yet, but we're working on that."

"We don't need retrofitted," I said. "We are both in excellent shape despite our ages."

"You'll have a neighbor on either side," she said. "Like you, they demanded quiet spaces."

Kate smiled. "May we see the rooms?"

"Yes. I do need you to be aware that when we are due to be inspected for licensure you'll be asked to move downstairs. There is one organization handling the licensing of over thousands of facilities in Georgia, so it won't be any time soon."

The old rooms were actually charming with high ceilings and crown molding.

"These are lovely," Maude exclaimed.

I looked out the window and down at what looked to be a small forest of pine trees. "I feel as if I'm in the country," I said. "Is there a set of stairs, a back door where we might slip out for a nice walk from time to time?"

The coordinator paled. "The back stairs are off limits I'm afraid. Too steep for some of our residents. You must use one of the central elevators. We do have a back door that you can reach through the lobby, but I don't recommend a walk in the back after dark—the ground is too uneven."

The woman seemed a bit nervous.

Kate stepped in. "I researched your facility. It comes highly recommended. Naturally, I want only the best for my grandmother."

I couldn't help but feel Kate enjoyed lingering on the word grandmother, emphasizing our age difference and implying I was some lovable old woman with an equally lovable companion.

Kate continued. "I heard about the recent accidents, and I assume that's why the back stairs are closed off."

"Yes. It was very upsetting. We know most of our residents will eventually move on to a more eternal facility if you know what I mean, but we don't want anyone to leave before their time."

"Well put," Kate said. "What did happen?"

"Two people fell down those back stairs. We don't actually know why they were in the area. Both had rooms on the second floor."

"Maude and I will certainly be careful about that," I said, and the woman smiled at us as if we were old dears.

"Our elevators are very reliable. Lunch is at noon in the main dining room and dinner is served at six."

She left us to settle in. Kate also left to check out our neighbors and the cordoned off back stairs.

"Nice room," Maude said. "High ceiling, crown molding. We should be very comfortable in here, Flo."

"Two single beds. I feel like I'm back in a dormitory." I bounced on one mattress. "Not as terrible as I expected."

Kate returned. "The notorious lounge is three doors down, empty at the moment, and the door leading to the stairs is locked. I'm happy about that. By law, I think they have to have egress other than the elevator. I'll speak with the coordinator about that. I checked out the names of your neighbors. You have a couple to your left and a single woman to your right. I wonder if they heard or saw anything."

"We'll let you know," I said. I was ready for Kate to get on her way, so we could begin a little detecting.

"I'm gone, Flo. You can stop acting so impatient. Alma will track you down at lunch and perhaps the three of you can take a walk outside the building. It's supposed to be a sunny day and close to fifty."

Alma stopped by our room before lunch. She was small and plump and looked like everyone's favorite elderly aunt. That was until she opened her mouth. Then she used a few words that almost made *me* blush.

"The situation is entirely out of hand," she said. "Two of my best friends have been murdered. Whoever did it knows I won't let it go as some stupid accident. They'll come after me next. They already have."

Before I could ask a question, she went on. A lot of anguish was pent up in that small body.

"The idea that Loretta and Bertholdt could be agile enough to have sex on an old sofa in a forgotten lounge and then tumble down a set of stairs is absurd." She didn't use the word 'have sex' or the word 'absurd'. Alma's language was much more colorful and to the point. "I'll find out who did this if it's the last thing I do."

"That's why we're here, dear," Maude said, "to make sure it isn't the last thing you do."

"And to bring a murderer to justice," I added.

It seemed as if all the air in Alma's tirade left her at that point. She sank onto the tiny sofa in our apartment. "I'm so glad you're here. I don't mind dying, never did. But the idea of dying at the hands of a killer who may never be caught is more than I can stand."

"Let's start with how you're being threatened," I said.

Alma looked around the room. "Is there any chance there might be cameras or recording devices in this space? They have them everywhere—except on the back stairs where my two friends died."

"Our assistant, Kate, checked out the room before we moved in. She found nothing," I said. "It's an old unused space, and we had to fight to be allowed to stay in it." I grabbed a jacket. "However, Kate did advise us that it might be safer to talk outside—no one listening at the door."

Alma nodded. We followed her downstairs to her first floor room. She grabbed her coat and a three-pronged cane, and we headed out the front door. "Just showing these newcomers the grounds," she said loudly to the receptionist.

Once outside, we walked around the building. Maude and I were blessed with good balance despite our ages and had no need for a cane. Alma relied on hers. "It's the Parkinson's," she said, "but the cane also makes for a good weapon. They can't throw me down the back stairs, so they'll make sure I fall here on the grounds and then make it look like an accident."

"Has anyone come after you in that way?" I asked.

"Yes. I always walk after dinner. A week ago it was dark, and the lights at the back of the house were out. It didn't bother me—I knew the path through the trees and loved the sense of being alone in the woods. I didn't see or hear anything. Someone shoved me against a tree—hard as they could. I started screeching. I don't think they bargained on my having such a voice— I used to sing with a small opera company.

"I was lucky. One of the aides was out back taking a smoke. He ran over to help me, and whoever planned to kill me took off."

"Did the aide see who pushed you?" I asked.

"No. He claimed he saw nothing and heard nothing but my screaming. He thinks I imagined the whole encounter."

"Well, that won't happen again," I said. "We'll ask Danny to keep an eye on you. He's a temporary aide here. Also a former policeman. He's helping us with the case."

"He's that hunk of divine masculinity I've seen around here?" Alma asked.

"Yes," I said, "but he's taken I'm afraid."

Alma chuckled. "A girl can dream . . . and remember the good old days."

"Yes," Maude agreed, "a girl can dream."

As we walked, we heard more about her friends Loretta and Bertholdt. Bertholdt's wife was in the Alzheimer's unit at the side of the building, pathetically called 'Mama's Memory Garden.'

"Bertholdt was devoted to his wife—visited her every day even though she sometimes didn't know him. But he was lonely. The three of us had come here about the same time, and we quickly became close friends. We ate dinner together every night. I could see what was happening between Bertholdt and Loretta and offered to find them a place where they could meet privately."

She pulled a handkerchief from the pocket of her coat and dabbed at her eyes.

"I'd wandered the halls when I couldn't sleep and knew

about the lounge that was never used at the back of the building. That's where they met, so I feel responsible for what happened."

"Nonsense," Maude said. She hooked her hand through Alma's arm and patted her. "You gave them happiness. I'm certain of that."

"If I'd let them get together in their own rooms, they might still be alive now."

"Why didn't you?" I asked.

"I'm sure you've heard about the STD epidemic in Florida. Our head administrator wanted none of that here. She instigated surprise bedroom checks. It was disgraceful, so I found a place where they wouldn't be discovered. That's what I thought."

"You don't think someone murdered them for having sex, do you?" I asked.

"I don't know. We have some crazy residents here. Some of them are strong enough to do harm. Bertholdt was a good-looking man in good health. He came mainly to be near his wife. We don't have many men, good-looking or otherwise. The women swamped him with cookies and cakes and all sorts of propositions. A few of them got jealous when he turned to Loretta."

"I have to ask," I said. "Did you have any feelings about him?"

Alma smiled. "If you mean, did I love him like a brother, yes, I did. But I was done with the rest. I was simply thrilled to see my two friends happy."

"How did Bertholdt handle it when Loretta died?" I asked.

"He was devastated, as was I. Then two weeks later he fell down the same set of stairs."

"Hmm," I said. "You don't think it could have been suicide?"

"No, I saw someone lurking around the lounge and the

back stairs before Loretta died. I didn't get a good look at the person, but Bertholdt would never have committed suicide, not after all he'd been through."

"All he'd been through?" I asked. "You mean his wife's dementia?"

"That and his troubled childhood. His parents died in the Second World War—that's what he told me. He said it gave him an appreciation for life. He'd never throw it away, no matter what."

"So," I said, "We could have a scenario where a woman in love with Bertholdt killed her competition, and then, perhaps rejected by Bertholdt, killed him as well. Could you see if it was a man or a woman near the stairs?"

Alma shook her head. "They seemed to be wearing a coat with a hood. I'm sure you've heard the rumors about me—that I'm seeing things that aren't there. I admit that sometimes happens. But not in this case. Berthodlt told me he thought someone was after him."

"Did he mention any names—anyone who seemed hopeful of a relationship with him after Loretta died?"

"No. He'd never have told me that, anyway. He was too respectful to embarrass any woman."

"It would have to have been a strong woman," Maude said, "if he was as vigorous a man as you suggest."

"It's true," Alma said. "But he was grieving. Someone could have caught him off guard. He went to the lounge a lot on his own after Loretta died—just to feel near her I think. I'd offer to go, but he wanted to be alone."

We'd reached the back of the building by this time, and the trees cast a shade over us. Even in bright daylight, the path through the woods was dark, and the ground under our feet was slippery from a multitude of leaves and a recent rain.

"I'm surprised they let you walk out here," I said. "You're positive you didn't stumble?"

"I'm positive," she said. "We walk here at our own risk. We sign a disclaimer. Folks in the nursing home or dementia unit can't get here. They have an enclosed courtyard.'

Alma showed us the spot where she'd been pushed into the tree. I pulled a flashlight from my pocket to get a better look at the ground and the tree. "The aide saw no one?"

"No," Alma said. "Of course, he didn't want to be reported for smoking on the grounds. It isn't allowed anywhere on the premises, except in that glass cage in the dining room."

I looked around the area. It had been a week with intervening rain, so I didn't expect to see much. It was Maude who spotted something. She picked up a cigarette butt near the tree and then another one.

"Was your aide smoking when he rescued you?" I asked.

Alma shook her head.

"I doubt he was the one doing this," Maude said. "Look— lipstick on the edges. These got buried under some leaves."

"The wind must have exposed them," I said. I brought out a plastic bag—something I'd seen real detectives do—and put the two butts into the bag.

"A woman," Alma said. "A strong woman." She showed me the bruise on her arm—now a faded purple.

"So, perhaps the jealousy theory is not too far off the mark," I said. "But why come after you?'

"I've let it be known I didn't think the deaths were accidental. The administrator told me I'd better be quiet about that or she'd have me out of here. Bad press. I quieted a little, but everyone knew I was looking for the person who killed my friends."

It was almost lunch time. We headed back to the front entrance and decided it would be best if we didn't look too chummy over lunch. Maude and I found a table half full of women about our age and asked if we might join them. Alma sat by herself at a corner table near the door. All of us were searching for smokers.

One corner of the room was designated a smoking area. It seemed if we'd reached this age, no one was concerned about getting a bit of lung cancer either passively or actively. We saw ten women and one man seated in the area. It was the glassed-off area Alma had described. So was our murderer among them?

Maude and I headed back to our room after a very mediocre lunch of mystery meat and overcooked vegetables. Once again I felt I was back in college. We agreed to meet up with Alma for a walk before dinner.

Once we entered the room Maude walked over to the kitchen area that held a small sink, a microwave and a miniature refrigerator. She turned the faucet on full blast.

"That's what they do in the movies," she whispered, "when they think the room might be bugged."

She spooked me, and I clicked on the TV, upping the volume loud enough for a deaf person to hear. Then we huddled close together on the couch.

"I saw you studying the people in the glass house," Maude said. "Did you see anyone who looked suspicious?"

"Anyone who smokes these days looks suspicious to me," I said. "There was one woman who looked out of place, as if she had just had her make-up done."

"I know the one," Maude said. "She looked younger than the others."

Someone knocked at our door, and we both jumped.

"It's me, Danny."

We opened the door, and he spoke loudly. "Could you turn down the TV, Miss Wells? The neighbors are complaining."

He stepped inside, turned off the TV and motioned us into the bathroom. He turned on the water in the sink and bathtub. "You're right to be careful."

"What do you know, Danny?"

"First off, I think they're trying to sell the place to a developer, so they don't really care what happens to the folks here. But they still don't want bad press. It's prime land, and the place will be torn down."

"Is that related to the murders?" I asked.

"I don't know," Danny said. "Rumor has it someone might have been skimming off money from the organization, hence the need to sell. I suppose it's possible the two were killed not for their relationship but because they saw something they shouldn't have. The lounge would be a perfect place for people to meet privately—not just lovers."

"Alma told us about her attack," I said. "Do you know about that?"

"I talked to the aide who found her. He suspected she was seeing things and simply lost her footing, fell into the tree. He said she'd been hallucinating and seemed paranoid about everyone. He blamed it on her Parkinson's."

"Do you trust him?"

"Don't know. He's pretty new, like me."

We told Danny about the cigarette butts Maude had found. "Alma didn't make that up."

Danny listened and nodded.

"Can you check on smokers here?" I asked. I handed him the plastic bag with the cigarette butts. "DNA?"

He laughed. "I'm not likely to get that—too expensive and time consuming—unless you find me a likely murderer. There's no chance of fingerprints after a week of rain. But maybe I can identify the lipstick. I'll see if Kate might recognize the shade."

"Maude and I both saw one woman a little younger than the others—in the smoking area. She might be in her early sixties. She was well-dressed, nice cut to her hair—black and streaked with gray."

"I know who you mean. She's come on to me as a matter

of fact. Makes it clear she has plenty of money and wouldn't mind a boy toy."

"Her name?"

"Melissa Wolf, if you can believe it."

"I'm not sure I do. Why is she here?" I asked. "If she has so much money, why would she live here?"

"That's a very good question. She claims it's temporary," Danny said. "A doctor told her she needed to alleviate her stress for a few months, live incognito, away from people who were causing her anxiety."

"That makes her sound like she's under witness protection or hiding out from gangsters," I said.

"It's possible."

"All right," I said. "It seems we need to make the acquaintance of Melissa Wolf or whoever she might really be. Get a cigarette from her. I suppose that means one of us needs to be a smoker."

Maude grimaced. "I hate cigarettes. I coughed up a storm the first time I tried one and I never tried again."

"Yes, it can't be you," I said. "It will have to be me."

"Hang on," Danny said. "I think I can set something up with her. She's interested and waiting for me to respond. Let me have a go first."

"Good. We'll check with our neighbors," I said, "to see if they've heard anything suspicious about the deaths or who might be using the lounge."

We split up after I told Danny to keep a close eye on Alma.

"I'm already doing that. I've told her to stay in her room or in very public places. No walking alone in the dark."

Danny left, and Maude looked exhausted. "Nap?" I suggested.

"Perhaps a short one."

I left her to it and decided it was time to meet our neighbors. I began with the woman to my right. She opened the door after I knocked two times.

"I'm so sorry," she said. "I saw that you'd moved in, and I meant to call on you this afternoon. I fell asleep instead. That seems to be all I do."

"My roommate, Maude, has the same affliction. I envy you. I'm up at all hours wishing I could sleep. My name is Flo, and you are?"

"Bette. As in Bette Davis. When I was younger people said I looked like her. Some said I had her same temperament."

I tried to imagine that, but it was difficult. She was a thin and fragile thing, and I couldn't imagine her bumping someone off in a jealous frenzy.

She invited me inside and waited until I was settled on a small settee at the foot of her bed. "It would take a freight train to wake me up at night," she said. "I worry about a fire. I might not hear the alarm and if I did how would I get out? The back stairs are blocked off."

"I wondered about those stairs. Doesn't seem that stairway should be locked."

"Then you haven't heard?" This time she whispered. "You don't know about the two tragic deaths? I wondered if anyone would move in here after that happened."

"I had heard something, but they told me it was an unfortunate accident. Do you think it was something more than that?"

Bette began to fidget. "I didn't see anything. Nothing." That she said quite loudly as if she thought someone might be listening.

Was everyone in this place paranoid or did they have reason to be afraid?

I leaned in close to her and whispered directly in her ear. "You seem frightened."

Bette took a pad of paper from the table and scribbled on it

— "I am." Then she ripped up the page and began to stuff it into her mouth.

Was I living with a bunch of psychos? I made her spit it out, wrapped it in a tissue and threw it away. Then I cleaned my hands with an alcohol sanitizer that I always carried in my pocket.

"Fine," I wrote. "We'll talk this way. What have you seen? What do you know?"

"Why should I trust you?" she wrote back.

This was going to be a tedious afternoon. I took her into the bathroom, turned on the faucets in the tub and explained who I was and why Maude and I were here.

"Thank goodness," she said. "I knew both Loretta and Bertholdt. A lovely couple. I didn't see Loretta fall, but I didn't think it was an accident."

"Why not?"

"What was she doing on those stairs? Bertholdt was always with her when she came or went from the lounge. He was a gentleman. I'd heard him warn everyone about those stairs—he'd never let her go up or down them if he wasn't at her side."

"Anything else?"

She hesitated.

"I need to hear everything."

"I don't want to get anyone in trouble."

"I never reveal a source."

"I've wondered about Alma."

"What?"

"I wondered if she was sweet on Bertholdt," Bette said. "She would bad-mouth Loretta from time to time. She said Loretta wasn't treating Bertholdt right—that she was taking advantage of him."

"Alma is the person who asked us to investigate," I said, "and how could Loretta be taking advantage of Bertholdt—two old people in an old people's home?"

"I always felt Loretta held something over Bertholdt—something to do with the war."

"The war?" I asked.

"World War II."

She now had my full attention. "What might that be?"

"I don't believe Bertholdt came here before the war. I believe it was sometime later under a cloud. That's the rumor anyway."

"You're saying he was a supporter of Hitler? That he was one of Hitler's Nazi Youth? That would be impossible. He'd have been too young for that."

"Not Bertholdt, but his father," Bette said. "The rumor is his father was a Nazi and Bertholdt's fortune came from art stolen from the Jews."

"Really?" was all I could manage. Here we were moving from a jealous lover to revenge for Nazi brutality.

"What exactly are you suggesting?" I asked. "That Loretta was blackmailing Bertholdt for her silence, that he finally wearied of it and pushed her down a flight of stairs? And then who killed Bertholdt?"

"I haven't gotten that far," Bette said. "Perhaps you should see who benefits from Bertholdt's death."

I left her, almost afraid to see what the couple on the other side of our apartment might have seen or surmised. I stopped in to see Maude. She was awake and ready for action. I filled her in on what Bette had told me.

Together, we knocked on the door of the couple next to us. The wife answered immediately. "Ah, our new neighbors, delighted to meet you. I'm Harriet. My husband, Gerard, is here somewhere. Gerard," she called. "Perhaps he's gone downstairs. Please come in."

We entered, accepted a cup of tea and chatted about the amenities the establishment provided. She seemed a few years younger than we were. "What brought you here?" I asked.

"Gerard and I were done with suburban living. It was time for someone to take care of us. We have no children, so we were on our own."

Maude nodded sympathetically. "I suppose that's what did it for us," she said. "That and the cold winters in Massachusetts. Flo has a good friend here who recommended we visit, see how we liked it. We like it fine. Of course, we didn't hear about the unfortunate deaths until after we moved in."

"Unfortunate deaths?" Harriet asked.

"You know—Loretta and Bertholdt."

"Seems I heard something about that," Harriet said. "I can't remember what exactly. I think there was an accident. Someone fell down the back stairs."

I wanted to ask her if she knew today's date, but I refrained.

Maude handled it. "I'm glad to be in a facility where I don't have to be responsible for anything. Honestly, I have trouble remembering the day of the week, sometimes the year itself."

Harriet's smile broadened. "I know just what you mean."

We were interrupted by Gerard. He burst into the apartment, full of energy. "I won, dear. Beat every last one of them."

"I'm so glad. What is it you won? Some people have come to visit. I'm sorry, I can't quite remember your names or why you came."

We introduced ourselves.

Gerard informed us he'd just won the ping-pong weekly championship. "Do you play?" he asked us.

We shook our heads.

"Have you had a nice time, dear?" he asked Harriet.

"Very nice. These people have come to visit us."

"We've moved in next door," Maude said.

"I see." Gerard said. "I think my wife may need a nap. I'll see you to the door."

He took us outside his apartment. "I hope my wife wasn't troubling. She's forgetful these days and sometimes says very strange things. It's one reason I insisted upon these rooms—so no one would bother her. I'm not speaking about you, of course."

"I understand," I said, "She didn't seem to know much about the two people who died. Do you?"

"Only a little. I haven't shared any of the details with her. Sometimes, she gets frightened."

"Do you know anything about the deaths?" I asked.

"Why do you ask? The police say they were both accidents."

"It's only that you are close to that lounge and the stairs. I wondered if you'd heard or seen anything that disturbed you."

"Nothing," Gerard said. He studied me. "We don't need any more busybodies around here. Has Alma been spreading her rumors? You need to be careful who you listen to, and if anyone is acting suspiciously about those deaths, I'd say it's Alma."

Here was the second person to throw Alma under the bus.

We left Gerard outside his apartment and headed to the lobby in search of Alma. We ran into Kate first.

"Grandmother," she said embracing me. "And Maude. I came for a visit. I was hoping I could take you out for a ride."

"We'd love that," I said.

We signed ourselves out, and Kate drove us to a handsome B&B in which she was staying. We talked in the car.

"Danny asked me about the lipstick. I matched it. *Love Divine* by Hillcrest. Expensive, not that it matters, except that it's in keeping with the woman Danny told me about. She calls herself Melissa Wolf. I think you wondered if that was her real name—it's not. She's actually Madeline Fox, heir to the Fox fortune, which has Hillcrest as one of its subsidiaries."

"And?" I asked when Kate paused.

"I believe you asked why she was here instead of a luxury facility in Buckhead?"

I gave her a blank look.

"Buckhead, the neighborhood in north Atlanta where the wealthy live. You wondered if she was part of a Witness Protection program?"

I nodded.

"You weren't far off the mark. Apparently, she left a brutal marriage, and she's here until she can find a more permanent home out of state."

"So what, if anything, does she have to do with the two deaths or with threatening Alma?"

"It seems Alma caught Madeline a.k.a. Melissa up to something with Bertholdt, and she didn't like it one bit. She told Madeline to back off. Apparently, no one tells Madeline to back off, hence the shove in the woods."

"How did you find that out?" I asked.

"Madeline opened up to me. I manufactured a story about my own need to escape a bad marriage and the rest came flooding out. She said she was afraid Alma would blow her cover. She claimed she was careful not to harm her—only wanted to scare her into keeping her mouth shut. She also said Alma was a terrible gossip, making up stories that harmed people."

"I'm wondering if Alma is not the sweet and frightened grandmother she claims to be," I said.

"Time for another chat with her?" Maude asked.

"I want to be with you when you have that conversation," Kate said.

We called Alma on her cell and asked if she could have dinner with us—somewhere away from the facility.

She sounded delighted. "You found something?" she asked.

"I'm not sure about that," I said, "but we need to talk."

In the meantime, we filled Kate in on all we knew and didn't know. She said she'd follow up on any financial problems the facility might be having. She also said she'd check on the background of Bertholdt. She dropped us back at the facility with plans to pick us up for dinner.

WE TOOK Alma to a quiet restaurant she recommended in Decatur. We sat in a back room and ordered tapas. It was early, so we had the place to ourselves.

It seemed simplest to be honest with Alma and observe her reaction. We told her about the two neighbors who were suspicious of her and the account that she told the Fox heiress to back off.

"Some of that is true, and most of it is not," she said. "That woman—she told me her name was Melissa Wolfe—she was a wolf and she came on to Bertholdt. He was too much of a gentleman for his own good. I told her to leave him alone. It seemed easier to suggest we had a relationship."

"There is also the rumor," Maude said, "that Bertholdt was the son of a Nazi."

Alma took a shallow breath. "I'm so sorry that has come to light. It's true, but Bertholdt wasn't responsible for the sins of his father."

"And yet he had wealth from Jewish art stolen during the war," I said. "Did you know about that as well?"

"Bertholdt didn't realize that until he was a grown man. Then he tried to find the rightful owners for the art that remained. It was a slow and difficult process."

"How do you know about all this?" I asked.

"He confessed it to Loretta and me one night. He said he

could no longer live with a lie. He had to keep enough money to provide for Ursula, his wife. Once she was gone, he would give the rest away to Jewish charities."

"How did Loretta react to that?"

"She was shocked. She was Jewish and had relatives who had perished in concentration camps."

"It was the first time she'd heard about Bertholdt's past?" I asked.

"Whatever made you ask that question?" Alma said.

"I'm not sure. You made them sound so close, and you made him sound like an honest man.

She paused. "There was something about the way Loretta responded that made me wonder. She almost seemed to be acting. She expressed her shock, of course, but she didn't act surprised the way I would have expected her to."

"So you think she may have already known about his secret past," I said. "Did her relationship with Bertholdt change after that night?"

"No. She seemed to get quickly over it. That also struck me as odd."

"I may be able to add something here," Kate said. "I've checked on the financial situation at the facility. It seems two big donors were keeping them afloat—the Fox Charitable Foundation and Bertholdt Schmidt. The Schmidt money stopped abruptly. That's why they had to sell."

"So one possibility is that someone was blackmailing Bertholdt," I said, "and that made his support dry up. One neighbor said he thought Loretta held something over Bertholdt. Could she have been blackmailing him?"

Alma looked dumbfounded. "I can't believe it."

"Can't believe it or don't want to believe it?" Maude asked gently.

"They were my two best friends. Why would Loretta do that?"

"Revenge is a powerful motive," Kate said. "If she had family killed during the war, perhaps draining Bertholdt's finances felt like the least she could do to make him pay."

"Can you check her bank accounts?" I asked Kate. "Talk to her next of kin?"

"No next of kin," Kate said, "but I did manage to find a friend of hers who made the funeral arrangements. He said she died with a considerable fortune and that surprised him. She'd never been a woman with a lot of money as far as he knew."

"Can we get any useful information from Bertholdt's wife?" I asked.

Kate and Maude shrugged.

"I've visited her," Alma said. "She's a lovely woman but very confused."

"A likely dead end there," I said. "And Madeline or is it Melissa? What does she have to say for herself?"

"That's Danny's department," Kate said.

She called him on her cell, and they spoke briefly.

"He'll catch up with us in our rooms," Kate said. "Lots to tell apparently."

We finished eating and returned to the facility. I asked Alma to stay with us and help us piece things together.

Danny found us in our apartment, and Kate caught him up on what we knew so far. He told us what was going on with Madeline. She'd been eager to meet with him again. When he started asking questions, she became a lot less eager.

The truth—according to Madeline—was that she'd come to the facility to escape a volatile husband. She had a trust that was supporting the facility. The place was always her refuge when she needed to get away. She had a suite in the back of the building on the ground floor where the original house had been located. Much of its grandeur remained for her exclusive use. Danny had asked why she'd chosen such a place.

At first she said it was because no one would ever look for

her there. Later, she admitted it was her grandparents' home before they made all their money in cosmetics after the war.

"Ready for this?" Danny asked.

We nodded.

"Her grandparents had fled Germany—Jews, who got out through connections. At first, she denied that she knew anything about Bertholdt Schmidt or his fortune, but when I pressed her, she changed her story. She'd heard he was also a survivor of the war and she wanted to meet him. She later discovered his family had been Nazis sympathizers. He was deeply ashamed of that and told her how he was making amends. He made sure the facility gave special dispensation to Jews in need as a condition for his financial support."

"She was satisfied with that?" I asked.

"No. She told him nothing would be enough until he was as destitute as her grandparents had been when they arrived in the US. She needed money now to escape from her marriage and demanded he give it to her. He did."

"That doesn't make a lot of sense," I said. "Why would she tell you that so freely? And how could her parents have afforded to build a grand house if they were in fact destitute?"

"I can't answer that one," Danny said, " but I think she told me the rest of it to prove she
hadn't murdered Bertholdt. He was her source of income that couldn't be traced to the family fortune. I believed her when she said she was afraid of her husband and the thugs he had around him."

"So, who did kill Loretta and then Bertholdt?" Alma asked. "And why?"

"So many threads lead back to the war," Maude said.

"A war that ended over seventy-five years ago," Kate said, "with all participants dead or nearly dead. Why now?"

"A dying wish perhaps?" I said. "A final act of revenge or

restitution? I wonder what Ursula could tell us about the enemies Bertholdt had."

I got blank stares.

"Maybe it would be a good idea to talk with her again. She might remember the past clearly even if the present is a blur. Anyone know about visiting hours on the Alzheimer's unit?"

"They're wide open," Danny said. "No one can leave the unit, but anyone can visit before ten pm unless they upset the patients. It's after eight—shall we go or stay?"

"Go," I said.

Danny nodded.

I stood. Maude, Kate, and Alma stood with me.

"Fine, we'll all go," I said. "If it's too much for her, some of you will need to stay outside."

In ten minutes we were on the unit, and the nurse in charge escorted us to Mrs. Schmidt's room. She told us we'd have to come back tomorrow if Ursula was asleep.

"Ursula—is she German?" I asked.

"Yes," the nurse said. "She and Bertholdt spoke only in German. With us, she says nothing, but she seems to understand what we say well enough. I've had questions about her diagnosis—she seems more aware than anyone else on the unit."

"How's your German, Kate?"

"A little rusty but not terrible."

She and I entered Ursula's room. Unlike the other rooms we'd passed by, this one was lovely with healthy plants lining a window sill, a colorful bedspread, and a small dog nestled next to Ursula.

She clicked off the TV when we entered and stared at us.

Kate spoke to her in German. No response.

"I told her we were friends of Bertholdt."

She looked past us and seemed to stare at someone standing in the doorway. "Alma," she said. "*Komm her.*"

Alma came in and hugged her. "These are all friends, Ursula. Friends of Bertholdt."

"That woman killed him, didn't she?"

"What woman? What's her name?" I asked. "Melissa? Madeline?"

She stared at me and then gazed again at Alma. "Who are these people?"

"Friends, like I told you," Alma said. "What woman do you think hurt Bertholdt?"

"That Loretta woman. She pretended to be my friend, and she killed Bertholdt."

"That can't be, Ursula," Alma said. "She died before Bertholdt."

"No. No! She pushed him. I saw it."

"You couldn't have seen it," Alma said. "You were never allowed to leave this place."

'Bertholdt took me out. Once. I saw her push him."

"You saw him die?" I asked.

Ursula lay back on the pillow. She looked confused. "Not die. But she wanted him dead."

"Why?" I asked.

"She knew his secret, our secret."

"What secret?" I asked.

Ursula closed her eyes. I was never any good about getting someone to trust me. But Maude was. I brought her in and introduced her to Ursula. Maude squeezed her hand. Ursula opened one eye and then the other.

They sat together in silence, Maude gently stroking Ursula's hand. After a minute, Ursula began speaking in German. Slowly. Kate translated in a whisper.

"It doesn't matter anymore. Bertholdt's dead. It was a terrible secret. Terrible. Not our fault. but we could never tell. We had to keep Papa safe."

"You and your husband, Bertholdt?" Maude asked.

Ursula shook her head. "Not my husband, my brother. Neither of us married. We were afraid of the bad genes. That was another secret. Bertholdt had me put in this unit to protect me, and I didn't mind. I wanted to stay away from the world anyway. Our past was too horrible."

Ursula's voice was no longer hesitant. She no longer sounded like a woman with Alzheimer's, and she began to speak in English.

"Is he really dead?" she asked. "My brother is really dead?"

"Yes," Maude said.

Ursula cried. "And it was not Loretta who killed him?"

"No, not Loretta," Maude said.

She cried harder. "Then Bertholdt did it. He killed Loretta to protect me. Then he killed himself."

Maude looked at me.

"Ask her why?" I mouthed.

"Why would he do that?" Maude said.

"He could see what would come next. Loretta's mother had died in our father's concentration camp—he was the Commandant and a wanted Nazi criminal. He died in hiding several years ago. Loretta found out that Bertholdt was his son and followed him here.

"She discovered I was in the Alzheimer's unit and visited me. She told me that she would destroy both of us and thought I was too far gone to tell anyone anything. What she wanted to do was frighten me. I pretended to be confused and said nothing. But, of course, I did understand. I told Bertholdt. He said it couldn't be true.

"He got me out of here one night—that other woman helped him. That Melissa woman—she knew everyone here. We confronted Loretta, and she confessed. She knew who we were. She'd kill us slowly. She shoved Bertholdt, but he didn't fall. And he didn't fight back. He said he understood."

Ursula lay back, eyes closed.

Alma looked at us from the end of the bed. "I can see it now—I couldn't before. It was Bertholdt I saw lurking by the lounge. He was the one who pushed Loretta down the stairs. When he had to choose between you and Loretta, he chose you."

Ursula nodded.

"And then he couldn't live with himself," Ursula said. "He kept repeating, *I'm as evil as my father.* No matter what comfort I tried to offer him, he couldn't bear it."

Ursula opened her eyes.

"He visited me the night he died. He told me he loved me and kissed me. Bad blood, he kept saying. I have my father's bad blood."

"Where does Madeline come into all this?" I asked.

"I think I know," Kate said. "There were two organizations funding the facility but under one umbrella. Bertholdt and Madeline knew each other. They knew each other's secrets— each claiming to be victims of the war, but in fact their relatives were Nazi sympathizers not victims."

"That would explain the money Madeline's family had and this mansion they built when they came to the United States," I said, "before their success in the cosmetic industry."

"Exactly," Kate said.

"So Madeline wasn't Jewish?" Maude said.

"No," Kate said. "I found that out in the research I did on the source of her fortune. Like Bertholdt's money, theirs also came from exploitation of the Jews. "

"My brother couldn't live with what our father had done," Ursula said. "He spent his life trying to give back the stolen art to its rightful Jewish owners. He gave money to this home, so it would be open to the Jewish community, to those in need. He and Madeline struck a truce. She would donate money to this facility as long as he never exposed her."

"So why are you so sure she wasn't the one who killed your brother?" I asked.

Ursula smiled, a small bitter smile. "She loved Bertholdt. When she said she needed money he gave it. Everyone who met Bertholdt loved him. I think even Loretta struggled with her feelings for him. She could have easily murdered me but I'm not sure she could have killed him."

Maude started to cry, and truth be told I wanted to do the same.

"There, there," Ursula said. "Poor Bertholdt was doomed. That was why it seemed better to pretend we were married. I knew what he was going through. He could never accept what our father had done. When he met Loretta, the wound opened up again. He loved her. I think she was the first person he ever really loved besides me. When she turned on us, he was broken. When she threatened me, he had to make a choice. He chose me over her, and then he couldn't live with what he'd done."

"How do we know it wasn't an accident?" I asked. "What exactly did you see, Alma?"

Alma squeezed her eyes shut. "I saw the two of them at the top of the back stairs. She'd come up behind him. It was dark. I couldn't see much. There was a struggle of some kind. He reached out to her—I don't know if it was to grab her or to push her down the stairs."

"So, we will never know," I said. "Nothing you've said about Bertholdt tells me he was a killer. Perhaps, he was trying to save her, and he couldn't."

"Perhaps," Alma said.

I turned to Ursula. "Do you really have any memory problems?"

She shook her head. "It's more often that I can't forget. My brother thought this was a safe place for me. I could have my little dog here, my flowers, and no one would bother me. He could visit me every day."

We left her. Was there any more to do about Madeline? She'd made her own fine mess, and she could live with it. Maude and I slept one last night in the facility. We had breakfast with Alma before we left.

"I'm sorry I brought you into all this. I didn't know what I'd seen or perhaps I didn't want to know."

"Will you be all right here, now?" Maude asked.

"Yes. I'll visit Ursula. Perhaps she'll move over here and stay with me. In any case, I'll have one friend."

"And Madeline?" I asked.

"It will be 'live and let live', " Alma said. "It isn't my fight. I wouldn't trade my life for hers—one in which she has to hide from a husband and her family's past.

I called Ditie to let her know all that had transpired. She offered her house to us once more but what I craved right then was my own space. I booked the three of us into the Whitley Hotel in Buckhead. That's where we spent our time before the 25th.

Ditie invited us for Christmas dinner. We planned to head home Christmas day, so we invited her for a Christmas Eve celebration instead, at the Whitley. She asked if her brother, Tommy, might join us with his partner, Josh. They lived close by.

The more the merrier was my feeling. We rented a large suite for the event and invited Alma and her granddaughter to join us. Maude and Kate had a field day decorating the space. I left them to it. I swear it looked like a forest of fake-snow covered Christmas trees by the time they were finished with a little glittery path among the trees.

The children—Lucie and Jason—were entranced and very well-behaved, I might add. Lucie brought a notebook and jotted down everything she saw. Jason went exploring with

Tommy and Josh, two delightful young men. Danny, Kate, Maude and I told our tales in great detail to Ditie and Mason. They didn't interrupt us once.

Over dessert, I brought up what was really on my mind. "I'm thinking we might expand our business," I said. "Have some affiliates. Kate says we are being bombarded with requests all over the country. Particularly in the South. It seems Southerners might bear more grudges than the rest of us."

Lurleen barely waited for me to finish. "We're no more violent than anyone else. We simply threaten people in more interesting ways and plan our murders a little more dramatically, perhaps."

"No offense meant, Lurleen," Kate said. "Flo is opinionated and doesn't speak for the rest of us. But we *could* use help. That's all she really meant."

Lurleen's hazel eyes sparkled with anticipation.

Ditie responded. "Before this gets out of hand, I'm sorry, but the answer is no. We are doing the best we can to manage our lives. We don't have the time or resources for your murder prevention work although I do admire it greatly."

Lurleen looked at Ditie and then at me. "Ditie may be too busy, but I'm not. I help her with all her cases. I've had this thought, Ditie, that it might be time to branch out on my own. With Danny here to help."

Danny grimaced. "I . . I get pretty busy," he said.

I could see I'd opened a can of worms. Even Lucie came up as I was speaking.

"You're talking about a franchise, a spin-off?" she asked.

"How old are you?" I said.

"Ten."

"You talk like a little adult."

Ditie sighed. "I'm trying hard to keep her in her child status a while longer."

I looked around at this group of eager and not-so-eager

participants in my plan. "Let's leave this tentative for now. Perhaps I can call on you if there is a need?"

"Yes, please," said Lurleen and Lucie in unison. They looked at me as if I were about to give them the most wonderful Christmas gift in the world. Ditie avoided eye contact.

"We'll be in touch," I said. Honestly, I didn't expect to mean it but something did come up in a few months, something in which I very much needed their help and Ditie's expertise.

THE END

ABOUT THE AUTHOR

Sarah Osborne is the pen name of a writer and physician who grew up in California, lived in Atlanta for many years, and now resides on Cape Cod. She is the author of the Ditie Brown Mysteries Series as well as a new series featuring octogenarians Flo and Maude.

She writes cozy mysteries for the same reason she reads them—to find comfort in challenging times. She also firmly believes that women of a certain age will one day rule the world.

Visit her on her Facebook Fan page: Sarah Osborne, Mystery Author and on her webpage: doctorosborne.com

Made in the USA
Columbia, SC
21 December 2022